DRAMA AT THE PALACE

DRAMA AT THE PALACE

VICTORIAN HEYDAY:
THE ALEXANDRA PALACE THEATRE
1873-1901

NIGEL WILLMOTT
AND
PATRICIA BREAREY

NORTH ONE COMMUNICATIONS
LONDON

Published by North One Communications Ltd
38 Denton Road London N8 9NS
For the Friends of the Alexandra Palace Theatre

Production by Treading Lightly
www.treadinglightly.co.uk

Printed by CPI Antony Rowe

ISBN: 978-0-9930727-0-3

Front Cover picture: The Theatre auditorium today
Back Cover picture: Detail of the Theatre ceiling today

Authors' note

This book began with modest aspirations to bring together in one place all the existing information about the Alexandra Palace Theatre, notably all the references to it in the only full-length history of the Palace by RC Carrington, some local history works, and various reports on the Theatre produced for repair and restoration work. Then we found a potential trove of new information in the local archives at Bruce Castle Museum and set to methodically mining them for new information. This soon widened to research in other archives, which became the underpinning for this history. This new research has allowed us to identify in large part, if not completely, the productions and performances in the Theatre, and those involved, both as performers, and creatively and technically.

Our original intention was to produce a complete history of the Theatre up until the present day, but the wealth of information, plus the need to input that information into the development of a lottery bid to regenerate the Theatre and east end of the Palace, led us to the decision to first publish a history of the Victorian years — the crucial period for the Theatre and its historic wooden stage. It doesn't pretend to be a definitive history: the more information we have uncovered the more questions have been raised. But it is, we hope, a good start in revealing the story of a great Victorian theatre, fully integrated into the mainstream of the mass entertainment industry of the age.

Contents

Introduction   11

The Theatre's first 25 years   21

The Performances   34

Pantomimes and spectacles 1875-76   45

Pantomimes and spectacles 1877-82   61

The Operas   78

Drama at the Palace   94

Variety and other events 1875-1900   119

Afterword   127

Introduction

On 7 March 2002, several score people in scarves and coats were welcomed to the Alexandra Palace Theatre by actor Juliet Stevenson from a temporary podium in the middle of the ruined auditorium, and afterwards listened to a short song recital in the gaslight effect of temporary lighting. The recital was short because without heating the damp from the walls soon began to chill to the bone.

But it was nevertheless a historic occasion: the first performance in the Victorian Theatre for nearly 70 years. During that time, the auditorium where actors such as Henry Beerbohm Tree, Lily Langtree and Gracie Fields strode the boards had spent 40 odd years as a prop storage area for the BBC. That was followed by 25 years of increasing dereliction, until it was saved by being listed, the decay was staunched, and a halting recovery begun.

The event was the launch of the Friends of the Alexandra Palace Theatre, set up as part of a project by the Alexandra Palace Trust to stabilise and recover the fabric of the theatre and bring it back into use. The event was made possible by work to replace the floor of the theatre foyer, ripped out because of rot in the 1980s, which once again gave direct access to the auditorium. Along with other measures, such as pinning the plaster ceiling, it was enough to gain a licence to hold small events there as a way of promoting the plans to revive the theatre.

The stellar cast on that night, which included actors such as Victoria Wood, Bill Paterson and Alison Steadman, produced a mood of optimism that the theatre could soon find a new life at the heart of a community rich in theatre professionals, musicians and performers. But as throughout its existence, the wider problems that beset the Palace intervened. Before it even got into its stride, the project was put on the back-burner. The financial position of the Palace, which had been close to breaking even in the first year of the decade, declined in the recession caused by the dotcom crash of 2001.

The longstanding plan of the trustee of Alexandra Palace, the London Borough of Haringey, to lease out the Palace to a developer was revived, after an administrative logjam of six years, leaving the long-neglected and near-derelict theatre with an uncertain future — if any — in any developer's plans.

But a spirit of hope against experience is part of the Palace's history, and in 2011 the chosen developer was despatched after a legal challenge to the tendering process. Haringey council started to put in place a new framework, developing its own regeneration plan for the Palace, including a bid to the Heritage Lottery Fund to revive the Victorian east end of the building. It will not be the final act in the theatre's eventful history, but it is one where the curtain might come down to appreciative applause once again.

The cycle of hope, failure and renewed optimism at Ally Pally was established right from the start. The Palace took 15 years from inception to its opening in May 1873, burnt down after 16 days, and was rebuilt and reopened in less than two years.

The idea of the Palace was inspired by the Great Exhibition of 1851, with its 6 million visitors and improving display of industry and innovation. The owners of Tottenham Wood Farm, a dairy farm on the eastern spur of the northern heights, sought to take advantage of the new northern railway passing through Hornsey and Wood Green with a scheme, published in a prospectus in 1858, for residential development and a Palace of the People.

But in a society sharply divided by class, which people exactly it was aimed at was to be at the heart of many of its later problems. The Rhodes family, relations of the empire-builder Cecil Rhodes, looked in particular to the success of the Crystal Palace — as the Great Exhibition's glass and metal Palace of Industry was dubbed by Punch — which was transferred from Hyde Park after the exhibition ended to a permanent site in south London, on the hills overlooking the city at Sydenham.

The 1858 Alexandra Palace prospectus began, according to RC Carrington in Alexandra Park and Palace — A History, the only detailed history of the Palace: "The Crystal Palace at Sydenham is highly prized by all classes of the community as affording, on a grand scale, the means of intellectual improvement and physical recreation."

It was to be all improving activities for the mind and body, with displays devoted to history, geography, astronomy, geology, mining and horticulture; and "archery, cricket, equestrian exercise and other amusements in the park". Clearly a prospectus aimed at Muswell Hill before the suburb even existed — with presumably something among the "other amusements" for the other side of the tracks in Wood Green and Tottenham. It was the kind of Reithian ethos later to be brought to the Palace with the BBC's television service — and one equally challenged later by the more populist ITV.

A grand design by Owen Jones, who had worked on the Crystal Palace, was published and a limited company set up in 1860, headed by Lord Brougham, who told potential investors that their success was assured, based on the returns for the Crystal Palace. The investors were not assured. Nothing more was heard of the Great Northern Palace Company.

1860 did see one interesting development though: the first public use of the land — a Ragged Schools Festival, bringing together what we would now term inner-city children, educated by the philanthropic Ragged Schools movement. One of the movement's leading lights, Henry Reader Williams, would play a key role in saving London's Northern Heights from over-development, with a green corridor running from Hampstead Heath, though Highgate Wood to Alexandra Park.

In 1862, another company raised the money to buy the land, proposing a 200-acre park (opposed to the original 150 acres). And in July 1863, a park was opened to the public in the name of another company, the Alexandra Park Company Ltd, which took its name from Princess Alexandra of Denmark, who had recently married the Prince of Wales.

The same month, the company stepped in to purchase most of the building that had housed the International Exhibition of 1862, a less successful version of the 1851 Great Exhibition. A deal was signed at the end of the year to use the materials salvaged from the Exhibition site for a building in Alexandra Park designed by John Johnson, with engineering and construction by Alfred Meeson.

At least, according to Carrington. Architect John Hutchinson's 1999 report to the trustees describes the first Palace building as "essentially the 1862-63 Cromwell Road Exhibition building given new Italianate facades by Alfred Meeson"; and the second palace as "an entirely different design by John Johnson, who had worked with Meeson". Whatever the division of roles between Meeson and Johnson, a construction company called Kelk and Lucas actually built the Palace, with an army of 12,000 men at its peak. Kelk and Lucas was to became directly involved as an investor in lieu of unpaid debts.

Preparatory work began, with plans for a cricket field, archery ground, tennis courts, a large gymnasium and a race course. Carrington quotes the response of the Illustrated London News: "We can now understand why the directors have adopted for the motto of their seal, Healthy Exercise — Rational Recreation."

However, the company's plans had missed the target with investors and the undersubscribed company was wound up in March 1865. But hope again vanquished experience and two new companies took over the project. The Muswell Hill Estate Company bought the land, while the other company, the Alexandra Palace Company Ltd, leased the land needed for the Palace and park.

The change of name was mirrored in a subtle change in the motto, from Healthy Exercise to Healthy Pastimes. Maybe a realisation that the new army of middle-class clerks might well dream of exercise on release from their desks, but the already well-exercised labouring classes looked forward to more relaxing diversions in what little spare time they had.

Building work continued apace, despite landslips, but the opening announced to the press in early 1868 failed to materialise. The opening of the Palace was delayed, waiting for the Highgate to Muswell Hill railway branch line to be completed. But the race course would hold its first meetings on June 30 and July 1 of that year.

The news was greeted sniffily by Baily's Magazine: "As a rule we affect not those gatherings to which the rabble of the slums and the cads of Cockneydom have easy access ... [but] If Alexandra Park becomes a gathering, great amongst the great, worthy to be talked of in the same breath with which folks speak of Ascot and Goodwood, we will be the very first to praise the ingenuity of those who evolved the happy thought."

Right up until the course closed a century later in 1968, folk never did talk of it in those terms — but it was the only part of the Palace and Park to reliably make money. Though as Carrington comments on the first successful race meetings, respectively drawing crowds of 40,000 and 50,000: "There can be no doubt that the affair was more successful as an opportunity for an outing than as an event in the racing world."

On the back of the publicity — good and bad — the company announced that the Palace would open on 1 May 1869 and tried to raise more capital. Once again, the pitch was high-minded, "to make the Palace and Park auxiliary to the great institutions of the British Museum, Kew Gardens and South Kensington in creating a taste for the study of the productions of nature, and of works of art and industry of all countries". But once again it seemed the public preferred Jack the Lad at the bottom of the hill to Samuel Smiles on the top. There was no new money and no 1869 opening.

In 1871, the directors tried a new approach to raise cash: a tontine — a kind of lottery, whereby the income was divided among the subscribers, increasing as they died off, until the last man standing took all. But this too failed and the subscriptions taken were returned. A new railways act provided hope that the branch line could be completed for an opening in spring 1872. But that date came and went also.

That was enough for one of the three development partners to pull out, leaving the contractor, Kelk and Lucas, and the London Financial Association to dig into their own pockets for the finance to complete the project.

While they sought to do that, the lord mayor of London tried to entice the wealthy burghers to pony up £100,000 to buy the Palace and park for the people. But the wealthy didn't get rich by investing in the social good and showed no interest. It turned out to be an idea several decades before its time.

As a writer in the North London News perceptively commented when the Palace finally opened: "I am glad to see that the cant about the 'Palace of the People' has been dropped. The Alexandra Park and the Crystal Palace are both shareholders' speculations in gigantic tea gardens and music halls of a superior description."

The Alexandra Palace Company complained about the lord mayor's interference and announced that plans to complete the railway were in hand and the Palace would open in spring the following year. It duly did on Saturday 24 May 1873, Queen Victoria's birthday.

The details of those first 15 years may be arcane, but the trials and tribulations embody all the issues that would dog Alexandra Palace throughout its history.

The First Palace

Johnson and Meeson's Palace building seems to have been conceived in clerical terms — reflecting, perhaps, both the Victorian gothic revival and the change from great religious to great secular buildings. According to Carrington: "The ground floor was basically cruciform with a nave 900 feet in length running east to west, and three transepts; a dome 220 feet high and 170 feet in diameter crowned the central transept."

The inner height of the dome of St Paul's is 225 feet, with a diameter of 102 feet.

In the western transept was a concert hall, while on the east side there was a theatre described thus by Carrington: "At the other end of the nave, the theatre was screened off from the rest of the Palace. Its large stage was only an inch or two smaller than at the Drury Lane

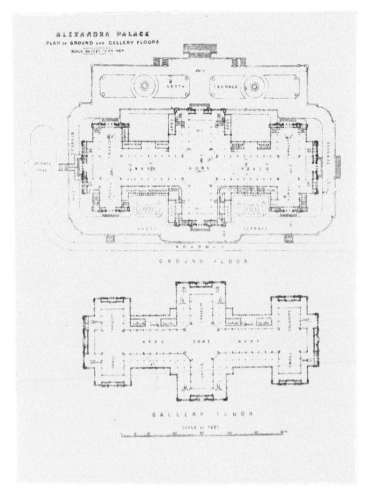

First Alexandra Palace: ground and gallery floor plans — Courtesy of Bruce Castle Museum (Haringey Culture, Libraries and Learning)

Theatre. The auditorium stretched in the south-eastern transept, and the galleries in the transept were to be used during performances. An orchestra pit had been sunk below floor level. Space 22 feet below the stage was kept for working machinery."

He goes on to quote a report in The Builder: "There are many features in this part of the building which have not been seen in this country before and the whole economy of the scenic art will be carried out, it is hoped, without that confusion, noise and delay which so disfigures the drama, even in many of our principal theatres. During afternoon performances the theatre will be darkened by an ingenious contrivance, thus allowing the various scenes to have their full effect."

Their full effect was never really felt: the Palace burnt down on Monday 9 June 1873.

The fire began around noon just after the Palace opened and it was destroyed in less than two hours. No visitors were killed, but three Palace workers died, including Thomas Larner, a foreman at the 1862 exhibition who had had helped rebuild the dome at Alexandra Palace. The subsequent inquest could find no evidence as to how the fire started in the dome, out of reach of fire hoses. A workman repairing leadwork was first put in the frame, but he denied it. Five painters were also working on the roof at the time. Once again, there are echoes down the years. A similar mystery surrounds the fire of 1980.

The financial problems of the Alexandra Palace Company and the speed with which the company met to decide to rebuild might have led to questions being asked. But it seems the Palace was underinsured, compounding the financial pressure on the company. Only £124,000 was paid out, nowhere enough to fund a new Palace. Fifty years later, new owners would face similar problems over inadequate war reparations — and 60 years later again, the insurance money would run out before the 1985 redevelopment was finished.

Even so, the day after the 1873 fire, a company meeting instructed John Johnson to provide a new design, with the aim of completing a new building within a year — a timescale that would make modern day developers call for every planner to be strangled with the entrails of every health and safety executive. But by the end of 1873 the foundations had been laid and the walls of the new Palace were starting to rise.

The Second Palace

Unsurprisingly, the new Palace building was not ready within a year. It was perhaps a tad ambitious even for Victorian builders and engineers. But the reopening in less than two years might still leave modern counterparts open-mouthed with envy and admiration.

Opening day, 1 May 1875, was appropriately wet and dismal. Carrington describes the building as "not so attractive as its predecessor. More solid, heavy and functional, it was obviously designed to be less susceptible to fire." It was to prove so for 105 years, despite two wars with aerial bombardment and a doodle-bug hit.

He continues: "This Palace was rectangular and provided more floor space. Fifteen million white Huntingdon and dark-coloured yellow bricks were used in construction. The central transept was crowned, not as before with a dome, but with a semi-circular roof." There were four towers, one at each corner, with a water tower at the top.

John Hutchinson sums up the building, which now had a north-south orientation, rather than east-west: "The palace had an area of 7.5 acres. It contained a Great Hall 125 metres in length by almost 60m in width. There was a concert hall seating 3,500, the theatre seating 3,000, a bijou theatre, a bazaar department 60m square, a banqueting suite 65m long overlooking London, library, lecture rooms, first-class restaurants, club rooms, a Palm Court, a small zoo, two picture galleries 60m long and a permanent exhibition space within the vaulted east entrance."

So far we know little about the bijou theatre, although it appears on plans into the 20th century.

The main feature — the central nave running north-south in the centre of the building — was the Great Hall, with its Willis organ and seating for 12,000, decorated in chocolate brown, lavender and grey. There were three east-west transepts and two conservatories (palm courts) at the western and eastern entrances, with two inner courtyards — on the west side an open Italian garden, the one to the east housing the exhibition space, installed late in the process to increase income.

The south of the building contained all the various refreshment rooms, sensibly placed for the views over London (unlike the 1985 development, which put its restaurant in the basement). Carrington also lists a room at the western end housing the Londesborough collection of arms and armour — remembered in the present-day Londesborough Room — and at the eastern end, Egyptian and Moorish villages.

All the building could be opened up to provide free flow of people, apart from the northern parts of the east to west transepts, where the concert hall in the north-west corner and the theatre in the north-east, were self-contained to reduce fire hazard. A wise decision then, perhaps, but one to cause problems for the theatre later.

It is also worth noting new features in the park, including three lakes to the north-west, a boating lake to the north-east with a water village on piles, a permanent circus building seating 3,000 near the lake, and close to the eastern entrance, a diving pavilion. The racecourse had a trotting ring added and a cycle track for racing. Near the Grove estate, in the west, was a Japanese village — possibly the origin of the dragons now in the theatre foyer, which were found in the lake when it was dredged in the early 2000s.

It is also worth noting that the park was bigger than it is now, with the Palace in the centre. The main entrance to the Palace was on the north side, from the station below the north wall, and via a tree-lined driveway where Avenue Road now is. Land north of the Palace would later be sold for housing to pay off debts.

Later changes — closing the station and moving the main entrances to the east and west — would add to the logistical problems for the theatre today.

According to Carrington, the "lord mayor, sheriffs and wardens of the principal companies drove in state from the Mansion House escorted by mounted police and a troop of the honourable artillery company" to the opening on 1 May 1875, and just days later, on bank holiday Monday, 90,000 people attended the Palace and park, putting enormous pressure on the rail system.

In December, the Alexandra Palace Company was able to announce a small profit for the first six months of operation. The directors deemed it the right time to cash in on their investment by selling the residential land at what they hoped would be twice the price they paid for it. But underneath the optimism of the opening season, there lurked the unresolved problem at the heart of the whole project, what we might call dodgy demographics.

As Hutchinson put it: "The developers intended to attract the well-heeled, leisured suburban middle classes from Highgate, Finchley, Hampstead, Totteridge and Barnet to frequent the building on a year-round basis, and to spend their money on the high-class cultural fare on offer. Instead they drew the new urban working classes in their tens of thousands, but only on Sundays and bank holidays, the available leisure time for these sections of society. Although the people in the huge holiday crowds had disposable income, it was modest."

Marlene McAndrew in Lost Theatres of Haringey puts flesh on the bones: "The average working day in the 1870s was 10-12 hours, six days a week, 6am to 6pm in factories, 8am to 8pm elsewhere ... According to one survey, average pay was 19s a week for men and 11s for women. The only leisure time working people had was the occasional bank holiday (only established after 1875, by act of parliament), and Sundays, when all forms of recreation and entertainment were closed, save for the church, the park and the pub."

In the circumstances, then, it was not surprising that a 1s combined rail and park entrance ticket was good value for working people of the inner city. McAndrew continues: "It was a great day if the weather was

fine. There was so much to see — balloonists, parachutists, re-enact-
ments of great battles, circus acts, bands, fireworks, races, a Japanese
village a race course etc. Families could picnic all day and let children
run around and play on the grass."

"Even in bad weather there were numerous attractions to enjoy
inside the Palace, but many of these had to be paid for separately, tickets
costing at least 6d — beyond the pockets of the masses — as were the
refreshment rooms.

"So it would seem that the rowdy poor stayed mainly outside, while
the refined middle classes patronised the inside, including the theatre."

The Theatre's first 25 years

The first Alexandra Palace Theatre

The story of the Victorian Theatre is one of tragedy and farce, interlaced with grand operatic interludes; of high ambitions and low pantomime — both on and off the stage. Little is yet known about the first Alexandra Palace Theatre, but it almost certainly embodied the ambitions and designs for the Theatre which succeeded it and survived.

The first Theatre was to be marked by tragedy even before it opened. The Tottenham and Edmonton Weekly Herald of 4 January 1873 reported on the inquest of George Hines, aged 42, who died while working in the theatre. "On Saturday last he was hoisted a distance of 95 feet to fix some poles in the roof of the theatre, when in commencing his descent he missed his footing and fell to the ground." The jury found no evidence "to show that the occurrence was otherwise than an accidental one".

The tragedy is laced with irony, because one of the innovations of the theatre was the "lock iron", invented by the stage designer, Thomas Grieve and Sons, to prevent accidents — but to actors falling below stage because traps were not secured.

As the Builder magazine reported, many of the features were new to the country and would improve the operation of the stage to avoid "that confusion, noise and delay which so disfigures the drama, even in many of our principal theatres."

Unlike the second theatre, the first ran north-south, at the eastern end of the building, in a "transept" to the central "nave", which ran east-west through the centre of the building. As Carrington described it, the stage was similar in size to the Drury Lane Theatre, "and the galleries in the transept were to be used during performance". It had an orchestra pit sunk below floor level and a 22ft undercroft below the stage for working machinery.

A report in the Weekly Herald in March 1873 describes the stage as being 85ft wide and 60ft deep, and the proscenium opening as 37ft high. It put the height to the gridiron floor above the stage — to which the scenery was attached — as 77ft and the height to the roof as 100ft.

The report goes on to describe lavish backstage facilities — in contrast to the later theatre. "The dressing rooms, wardrobes, retiring rooms, offices, lavatories, and other conveniences are at the rear of the stage, from which they are divided by a partition wall and corridors extending across the entire width. They consist of the ground floor and the storey above, approached by spacious staircases."

Carrington places the theatre in the south-east of the building, but both the Herald report and the Alexandra Palace Programme of Arrangements for 1873-74 place it in the north-eastern part of the building. The AP booklet puts the depth of the stage from the footlights to the back wall at 52ft and the width of the proscenium opening at 36ft.

The Weekly Herald reported on the stage décor. "The front of the stage on each side of the proscenium will be handsomely decorated. Ornamental pilasters and mouldings in Portland cement with carved capitals, will be carried up to a considerable height above the proscenium, an archway springing from the capitals. The space in front, between the proscenium and the archway over it, will be filled by a large fresco, executed by Mr J Absolon, of the Society of Painters in Water Colours."

This is confirmed by the AP Programme, which gives the credits for "a most complete and perfect theatre" as being "from the designs of Messrs T Grieve and Sons, under the superintendence of Messrs Meeson and Johnson, the Company's architects", in a building "erected by Messrs Kelk and Lucas". It adds: "The proscenium arch has been decorated by Mr C Schmidt and Mr John Absolon."

According to another newspaper report, "on each side of the theatre are colossal statues of Thalia and Melpomene" — the Greek Muses of comedy and tragedy respectively. Whether that means at each side of the stage is unclear.

The theatre in both its incarnations may have hosted many of the leading performers and actors of the day, but the same report on the opening day of the first Palace, 24 May 1873, makes clear the real star of the theatre from the very start: the stage itself.

"No performance took place on Saturday [24 May], but the drop scene was raised and a very pretty woodland scene, by Messrs Grieve, was exhibited. Not a few remarks were made about this. Everyone admitted the beauty of the scene …"

At the moment, we have a record of only one performance in the first theatre, on Monday 26 May — a dramatic spectacle with "Mlle Rita Sangalli, the premiere danseuse of the Grand Opera, Paris". The young Italian ballerina, Rita Sangalli, then in her early 20s, had made her debut at La Scala in her teens, toured America and appeared at Her Majesty's Theatre in Haymarket before settling in Paris. Whatever the spectacle was, it suggests high artistic ambitions of some kind.

The AP Programme of Arrangements for that opening season describes the purpose of the theatre as for "operatic and dramatic performances". However, before that purpose could be realised, a dramatic event of operatic proportions intervened: the Palace burnt to the ground on 9 June 1873, just 16 days after it had opened.

The Theatre was to play a leading support role. According to the Illustrated London News, quoted in Carrington, the fire was started by a "morsel of red hot charcoal" dropped by workmen repairing lead work in the roof of the Great Dome. "In a few minutes, almost before the alarm could be given, the central part of the dome, inside as well as outside, was enveloped in flames, which quickly spread in every direction till the whole vast building was consumed."

The same report added: "Nothing is left of it but the blackened ruins consisting of some portions of the walls, the two end gables, and the gables of the three transepts. This disaster was the work of an hour and a half to two hours between noon and two o'clock."

This was a drama, in less than the time of a three-act play, that all the scenic conjuring of Grieve's stage machinery could never have matched. Another newspaper reported: "Dense volumes of smoke still rolled upwards especially from the ends, where the theatre and concert room [in the north-west transept] afforded more fuel for the flames than was furnished by the body of the building."

The fire claimed three more lives, all Palace workers. Richard Jordan was fighting the fire with pails of water when the dome fell in and he was buried. The foreman of the caterers, John Kelsey, was trapped in the plate room, and Thomas Larner was killed in the grounds, some 50 yards from the building, when he was struck by large burning framework carried from the area of the theatre in the north-east of the building. The inquest on the men was unable to reach a verdict on what had caused the fire.

The first Alexandra Palace clearly was a stunning building. The Palace was then situated in the centre of the park — the land to the north would only be sold off for housing later — with all parts of the building interconnected to allow a free flow around all the entertainments and exhibitions. It also appears that visitors could walk all round the building along the galleries, affording spectacular views of the countryside all around.

But that openness came at a cost when the fire hydrants failed and the fire spread unhindered throughout the whole building. Some of the precautions taken for the second theatre would also hamper some of the original ambitions.

The second Theatre

The Victorians were unlikely to be daunted by the small matter of their main asset burning to ground. The Alexandra Palace Company met on the very afternoon of the fire and decided to continue the programme of outside events, while a meeting the next day instructed the architect, John Johnson, to design a new building to be finished within a year.

In the period following the fire there was much press comment about safety. The Builder commented: "The directors have paid a heavy penalty for economising the salary of an engineer." And the Graphic wondered what might have happened if 40,000 visitors had been in the Palace and whether there should be more exits other than the paying barriers.

In the aftermath it also emerged that the directors had under-insured the building, as well as skimping on safety — adding to the financial problems of the company which had just lost its main source of income. So if the second building lost some of the panache of the first, it's not surprising, given the need to concentrate on safety and rebuild as quickly as possible.

The second structure, which already had its foundations laid by the end of 1873 by Kelk and Lucas, the contractor, would be a more functional building, even if the Alexandra Palace Company's report earlier in the year had promised "that the building will be one which, for beauty of design and aptitude for the purpose it is intended, has probably never been equalled". A promise to be taken with the same pinch of salt as the company's financial forecasts.

A report in the Weekly Herald in May 1874 gave an equally exulted view of the theatre under construction. "Within the Palace will once again be a large theatre, as perfect in its construction and appliances as that which was destroyed last year. It will be capable of accommodating about 4,000 persons, and the nature of the performances will be such as to suit all those dramatic tastes which are not too low to merit cultivation."

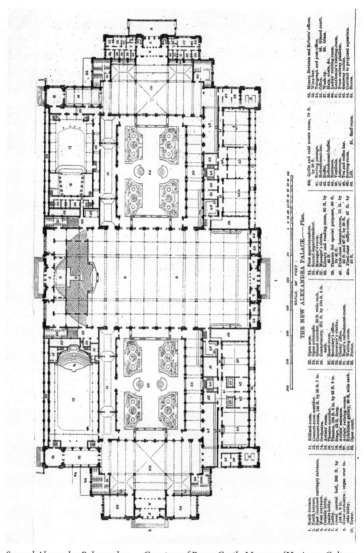

Second Alexandra Palace: plan — Courtesy of Bruce Castle Museum (Haringey Culture, Libraries and Learning)

By April 1874, 1,800 men were at work on the building. The attention to fire safety did not extend to the construction work and more workmen were killed in two accidents in the early part of the year. By the summer of 1874 the company admitted the work would not be finished that year.

The second Alexandra Palace finally opened on 1 May 1875, six weeks shy of two years since the first Palace burned down — a more realistic timetable for a seven and half acre building, but still remarkable.

Carrington describes it thus: "Seen from the park, the new Palace was not so attractive as its predecessor. More solid, heavy and functional, it was obviously designed to be less susceptible to fire. The first Palace was a long narrow nave intersected by three transepts which projected each side; this Palace was rectangular and provided more floor space. Fifteen million white Huntingdon and dark-coloured yellow bricks were used in construction.

"The central transept was crowned not as before with a dome, but with a semi-circular roof. There were four towers, one at each corner of the Palace, and at the top of each tower was a tank containing 16,000 gallons of water as an aid to fire fighting ... It was no longer possible to promenade right around the Palace as no terrace was provided on the northern side."

The theatre which emerged was also in the north-east of the building, but aligned east-west, rather north-south as in the first theatre, with the stage to the west, rather than the north.

It was claimed a fire starting in the theatre could not spread to the rest of the building. A brick corridor some 8ft wide and the length of the theatre was built to its south. In another nod to Victorian medievalism, it has high buttresses which would not be out of place in a Norman castle.

The Alexandra Palace Programme of Arrangements 1875-76, gives the basic dimensions of the stage, once again designed by Thomas Grieve and Son. The proscenium opening was 36ft wide and 32ft high, and the stage, 50ft deep by 84ft wide. The capacity is given as 3,000 people. Building News put the length of the auditorium from the back to the proscenium at 104ft 6in.

Above the stage it describes two tiers of flies, to haul the scenery up towards the grid, at 25ft and 37ft respectively; with the grid-iron floor, which carries the blocks, or pulleys, through which the fly lines run, at 49ft (much lower than for the first theatre, which had the grid iron floor at 77ft above the stage).

Beneath the stage, the cellar was 22ft deep, and described as being "capable of receiving the heaviest set scene". The stage itself is described as having five bridges — walkways beneath the stage, perhaps with rising platforms — each 36ft long and "a large number of working cuts" — the apertures through which scenery is lifted on to, and lowered from, the stage.

Behind the stage, to the west, were dressing rooms, wardrobe and other apartments, divided by a partition wall and corridor.

The AP booklet again describes the use of the theatre as for "operatic and dramatic performances", and gives an outline of the plans for the first season. Most notable is the engagement of the Carl Rosa opera company for a regular season of operas in English.

"Feeling the importance of producing operas in English in the most complete and efficient manner, the Directors have entered into an arrangement with Mr Carl Rosa, who has been for some time engaged in England and in Italy in forming an Operatic Company of the highest class, which will comprise many leading English artistes, with the addition of others who will appear for the first time in this country.

"These operas will be given in the Theatre in the months of September and October. The Company will be precisely the same as that which will appear during those months at the Princess's Theatre, and the Operas will be supported by a numerous Chorus and Ballet. The repertoire will include two Operas new to England."

It added that during May, "Opera Comique and Ballet Divertissement" would take place in the Theatre daily except Saturdays. So far, then, very much tending to those "dramatic tastes which are not too low to merit cultivation".

A newly discovered report in the newspaper The Era (9 May 1875) reveals the details of the very first performance in the second Theatre — and also provides some highly illuminating comments on the Theatre itself. The report indicates that on the opening day of the Palace, Saturday 1 May 1875, the Theatre "was not even ready for a theatrical representation".

However, on the following Monday (3 May), there was "a light, attractive, and thoroughly suitable entertainment … in the shape of an operetta and grand spectacular ballet". The operetta was Jacques Offenbach's Breaking The Spell — appropriate perhaps for a building said to have been cursed by an old Gypsy woman who lived on the hill on which it was built. The operetta was followed by the Alexandra Palace Theatre's own creation: Minerva, The Tutelary Goddess Of The Arts And Sciences.

One great advantage, The Era thought, was that the performances were not too long. "Now that bright sunshine, full-foliaged trees and lovely flowers tempt the Londoner to visit Muswell Hill, the charming grounds will naturally become an attractive feature, and, without disparagement to the Theatre, it may safely be concluded that a pretty operetta lasting about an hour, with a brilliant ballet occupying a similar period of time, will be quite sufficient to make the necessary variety in the programme."

The writer found the Theatre "large and lofty" and added that "to those accustomed to the Metropolitan houses will appear remarkably wide". Which is an interesting comment given that the general consensus about the theatre is that it is much too long. "The great width will enable a much larger number to hear and see well," the review concluded.

It goes on to declare the Theatre a "complete success, for, taking our places in various parts of the house, we found there was little perceptible difference in its acoustic qualities, and even at the extreme end of the building the singers in the operetta could be heard with the greatest distinctness."

But it adds an important coda, "although of course there was some diminution of effect in the dialogue" — reinforcing the view that the theatre was better suited (and perhaps designed for) spectacle and musical theatre rather than spoken drama.

It notes the two balconies "of graceful curve" and importantly adds "which, unlike similar erections in London Theatres, do not reach so far as the proscenium".

It then makes important observations on the sight lines and lighting. "The area is simply vast, and the gradual rise from the stage to the back of the house is such as to afford every individual spectator a good view of what is going on upon the stage. The lighting is arranged by circular gasoliers suspended from the ceiling, a great improvement upon the objectionable 'sun lights' now so much in fashion, but which to our thinking utterly destroy the charming effects of colour and the agreeable diffusion of light and shade which used in old times to be a graceful characteristic of the auditorium.

"The side windows, which light the Theatre when no performance is going on, are during representation blocked up with dark screens."

It also adds useful information on décor, revealing that the "act drop", the proscenium curtain lowered and raised between acts, showed "a classical pile of antique buildings". It adds with approbation that the "decorations of the Theatre are of a more subdued character than in other portions of the Palace". Unfortunately, it gives no more detail, though it does add that on each side of the "almost square" proscenium there was a statue in a recess — of Thalia and Melpomene resurrected perhaps.

The Era was more critical on the "important subject of ventilation", of which "some improvement may yet be made. The Theatre was certainly rather hot during the performance."

Breaking The Spell, which saw the first performance at the Palace by Richard Temple, who would develop important links with the Theatre, was judged by The Era to be "well adapted for the occasion, and went uncommonly well". Of Minerva, it noted features "of a novel and pleasing character, quite different from the ordinary ballet" and concluded: "Its success was complete, and it will undoubtedly attract the bulk of the visitors to the Theatre during its representation" — suggesting it ran throughout the month.

The Whit Monday bank holiday (17 May) was the first key day in the calendar for the Palace. On bank holidays it could attract thousands, often tens of thousands, to the day's events. According to the Weekly Herald, 94,125 people passed through the turnstiles that first holiday.

It was a packed programme in the Theatre. The day began at 12.30 with a new operetta by Louis Diehl. At 17.30 there was The Area Belle, a farce by William Brough and Andrew Halliday. Following each of these performances was the "New Grand Spectacle" — Minerva. Minerva, according to the Times, "descends from Heaven and creates the Arts and Sciences; the transition from barbarism to civilisation is effected before our very eyes".

Minerva seems to be basically a series of tableaux of a slightly idiosyncratic selection of the most influential practitioners of the arts and sciences, from Homer and Archimedes, through to Newton and Wren. It too had a premiere danseuse, "Mdlle Virginia Milani from Scala Milan". But the credits perhaps give away the real stars: new scenery is credited to Messrs T Grieve and Son, machinery to Mr Littlejohn and lime light to Mr Cox, gas engineer.

According to the Weekly Herald, both performances "were witnessed by large and enthusiastic audiences, who loudly applauded some of the tableaux, and went into ecstasies at the dancing of Mdlle Milani".

Whether such a spectacle was high or low art is difficult to judge with hindsight. It might seem cheesy to modern tastes, but the Victorian age seems to have had much more blurred distinctions between elite and popular taste. Dickens may now be seen (not by all) as part of the canon of English literature. But Dickens was undoubtedly a popular writer read in widely circulating magazines. And Dickens himself was an avid theatregoer, not with any great distinction as to what he watched.

Shakespeare was cut, edited and rewritten for a popular audience, and opera was still a form of popular entertainment, not quite yet

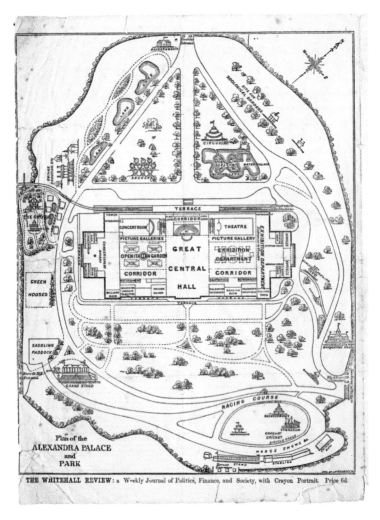

Second Alexandra Palace and Park — Courtesy of Bruce Castle Museum (Haringey Culture, Libraries and Learning)

elevated to a metaphysical plane by the influence of Wagner. Opera sung in English is perhaps also part of the same lack of purism, as well as being a staging post on the road to the 20th-century split between grand opera and the popular musical.

The respectable Victorian concept of wholesome entertainment would become more stretched when the first pantomime was produced at Alexandra Palace at Christmas 1875, not to mention the appearance in the theatre of music hall artists — which it seems was the kind of entertainment that was considered to be too low to merit consideration by the founding fathers. But Victorian respectability was always dosed with a liberal sprinkling of hypocrisy.

It's this mix of performances that is worth looking at in more detail to gauge the full range of the popular entertainment provided in the Victorian period at the Alexandra Palace Theatre: spectacles and pantomime; opera and operetta; drama, including farce; dance; and variety, burlesque and music hall acts.

This era in the theatre spans the last quarter-century of the Victorian age. The Palace as a whole was a home for almost all the popular forms of entertainment of the age. But the theatre fell foul of the unviable economics of the Palace, which could pull in huge crowds for some days — bank holidays, high summer weekends and Christmas — but failed to find a business model that would work year round to pay its huge overheads.

So the theatre, along with the rest of the Palace, suffered long periods of closure and inactivity as successive managements tried and failed to make a profit.

The first great hopes for the People's Palace had already faded by 1876, when the Alexandra Palace Company filed for bankruptcy, with the Palace offered for auction — unsuccessfully — in February 1876.

Carrington lists three reasons for the failure of the company. First, 10 years of heavy expenditure, without any income to pay interest on mortgages and debt. Second, the fire which destroyed the first building, with the consequent further loss of income and the extra rebuilding costs due to under-insurance.

Third, was the very conception of the enterprise: "It was typical of Victorian enterprise that they thought and built in spacious terms. Extensive grounds with many attractions and buildings meant that money had to be spent to maintain the park in attractive condition. A large Palace, covering over seven acres, also brought maintenance and financial problems. It was evident that a normal damp English summer was a handicap, that the winter months were disastrous, and the simple fact was that it did not pay its way."

He concluded: "The first palace was in smoking ruins in 16 days; the second in financial ruins in just over 16 months."

Most succeeding owners, trustees and managers would struggle to do better.

The next 25 years were to be a history of hope against experience, as a number of lessees believed they could beat the odds, if only for a summer season. The bookmaker always won.

The first manager of Alexandra Palace (at least of its second incarnation) was Sir Edward Lee. In November 1876 he published a pamphlet in his defence as manager, heavily criticising the Alexandra Palace Company.

"We may safely say that in the whole history of joint stock companies ... one has seldom to record so humiliating a story." He blamed the company for being "overweighted with capital" and failing to make use of its 280 acres of eligible building land. He said it was impossible for the Palace, the only income-generating part of the company's assets, to make sufficient profit to pay for the company's heavy financial costs.

But he concluded, according to Carrington, "with cheering affirmation" on the prospects of Alexandra Palace in the right hands: "Its popularity and money-making capabilities are beyond question, and with judicious, independent, energetic and liberal management, an efficient staff and a reasonable capital, it undoubtedly possesses the capability of being made a financial success."

Modern managers have also optimistically taken up the reins on this basis.

The reality was that of the lessees after Lee, William Henry Jones and Benjamin Barber, were to be the longest lasting — just over two and a half years. The Palace would be closed for long periods of the year, usually through the winter with the exception of Christmas. And would see complete closure between September 1882 and March 1885; August 1885 and April 1887; and a final eight-year closure from 1889 to 1898.

Carrington sums up the situation after the failure of the final lessee, Thomas J Hawkins in 1899: "In the first 25 years of its life, the palace was open to the public for less than half that time — in all for a little over 10 years. Eight different managements tried to make it a success. Two took the lease for the summer period only but did not return the following year — or ask for a longer lease. Of the remaining six, five went into liquidation."

Though Carrington precisely enumerates the managements who tried to make the Palace work as a private business, it is harder to identify exactly who they were. And then it is unclear whether the general managers also ran the theatre, or if that was delegated.

From current sources it seems that the lessees/mangers were:
Alexandra Palace Company / Sir Edward Lee, 1875-76
Messrs Bertram and Roberts 1877-79 / WH Jones

Mr Willing (Willing & Co) 1880 / WH Jones
William Henry Jones and Benjamin Barber 1880-82
George Collins Levy and Edgar Ray 1885
Alexandra Palace and Park Company 1887-89 / HW Hayward
1887-88
Alexandra Palace and Park Company 1889 / S Lee Bapty
London and Middlesex Freehold Estates Ltd 1896-1900 / Thomas
J Hawkins 1898-99
London and Middlesex Freehold Estates Ltd 1900-01 / Mr EA
Hearn.

None of them is exactly a household name — and once again their various backgrounds illustrate the clash between high-minded aspiration and populist reality. Sir Edward Lee had been knighted for his work as director of the Dublin exhibition in 1872 and went on to become managing director of the Albert Palace. But, on a rather less elevated level, he was tried for fraud in 1899 (though found not guilty).

Bertram and Roberts were the caterers under Lee before taking on the lease, while virtually nothing is known of Willing, except that he was an advertising agent. WH Jones seems to have been an energetic manager of the Palace — but died, six months after his company went into liquidation, of heart disease, said to have been worsened by his stint at the palace. Benjamin Barber was another refreshments manager turned lessee.

From what little we know of the rest, George Collins Levy was an Australian involved in politics and exhibitions in Australia, and Samuel Lee Bapty appears to be an exhibition organiser (including the Edinburgh Exhibition of 1890).

Despite all their efforts, Alexandra Palace finally passed into public hands in February 1901. Just weeks before, Queen Victoria had passed on to a better place, after a reign of nearly 64 years.

The Performances

The mix of mainly drama and opera in the Alexandra Palace Theatre holds through every period of the Victorian years, apart from the very last couple of years, when variety and audiovisual shows — perhaps presaging the coming entertainment form — took over as the main attractions, mainly, it seems, because of licensing problems caused by the deteriorating state of the theatre.

Mostly the productions seem to have been mounted by touring companies, often with West End transfers or adaptations. The main exceptions appear to be the pantomimes and spectaculars, which are almost certainly the distinct theatrical contribution of the Alexandra Palace Theatre — productions in which the stage would play a major role.

Pantomimes and spectacles

Many leading performers of the late Victorian age appeared at the Alexandra Palace Theatre, from popular entertainers, to leading actors, prima ballerinas and music hall artists. But there was really only one star: the stage itself. And the showcase for the star act was the pantomimes and other spectacular entertainments mounted between its opening in 1875 and the start of its long decline in 1882, when the Palace succumbed to the unviable economics of a huge seven and a half acre pleasure palace on top what was still a relatively remote semi-rural hilltop.

The 1870s were not quite the heyday of Victorian pantomime, which was to come later under the regime of Augustus Harris at the Drury Lane Theatre in the 1880s and 1890s, but it was already the most spectacular and successful of popular entertainments, and a money-spinner for the expanding theatres. The development of pantomime and spectacular theatre was fuelled by the end of theatre licensing, a growing urban audience, especially among the new working class, and rapid developments in technology; factors that were uncannily replicated a century later in the growth of the "industrial theatre" associated with Andrew Lloyd Webber.

The conflict between middle-class aspiration and working-class populism at Alexandra Palace has already been noted. Until 1843, it was enshrined in law. Under the Licensing Act, only two theatres in London had royal patents that allowed them to perform spoken drama: Drury Lane and Covent Garden. But increasing demand from London's rising population for theatrical entertainment meant a growth in "non-patent" theatres, which performed dramatic scenes interspersed with musical interludes to escape the restrictions.

The developing forms of melodrama — a term first coined in the early 1800s — and burlesque (early in the 19th century the terms seem to be almost interchangeable) became so popular that the patent theatres even began to perform them. In the 1830s the burlesque — and later pantomime writer — JR Planche satirised the situation in a sketch with three characters, Mother Drama and her two sons, Legitimate Drama and Illegitimate Drama. In 1843 what had become a legal farce was ended when the Licensing Act was repealed and all theatres could perform spoken drama.

What happened next was what we would call today a mash up, with "legitimate" theatre cutting down Shakespeare and adding more spectacle, and "illegitimate" theatre adding storylines (however improbable) to melodrama and burlesque to create farces and pantomimes and new popular forms of theatre where spectacular stage effects were as important as the narrative.

It is in this context that the Alexandra Palace Theatres were built. The owners of the Palace might profess to want productions of opera and drama and avoid entertainments of the lowest kind, but it's hard not to see the state-of-the-art stage as built for these new forms of theatre. Though information about the intentions of the designers is scarce, the Theatre's proportions — too long for spoken plays to be heard clearly at the back of the auditorium — appear more suited to spectacle and music than to the declaiming of Shakespearean verse.

In any case, what the owners of Alexandra Palace classed as "low" was specifically music hall and its risqué culture and mores, not the "uplifting" spectacle, such as the opening production of Minerva or the new domestic melodramas based on real life events, with enough moralising to placate middle-class sensitivities. And if pantomime, with its female principal boys in shorts displaying an uncommon amount of lower limb, and its sly undermining of authority, was not quite as uplifting as it should be, it did pay the bills.

Many comparisons were made between the Alexandra Palace

Theatre and Drury Lane — in terms of overall size (if not proportions), seating capacity and the size of the stage. So it seems reasonable to assume that the West End theatre was a model. Indeed Thomas Grieve of Grieve and Son, which built the stage, made his name at Drury Lane. His son Thomas Walford Grieve added new developments to the Alexandra Palace stage, such as the lock-iron. The theatre may not have been built to compete in a commercial sense with Drury Lane, but Alexandra Palace may well have hoped to equal or surpass it in technical achievement and spectacle.

The theatre landscape of the 1870s was very different from today. It was all commercial and still dominated by touring companies, as it had been since the days of the Commedia dell'Arte troupes which appeared in the 17th century, performing street theatre in market squares, then moving on. Roles were much less defined. The famous actor-managers of the age were both artists and businessmen. Theatre managers were often actors and involved in productions, and writers, directors and stage technicians might also appear on stage.

Theatre was also very much a family business, with whole families, male and female, adults and children involved, often working together, passing on the skills through the generations. Public-supported repertory theatre and drama schools were yet to come.

And the borders between different styles and formats — classical drama, melodrama, farce, burlesque, variety, pantomime, spectacle, dance, opera, opera-bouffe — were fluid and often intermixed, as on the bank holiday theatre programmes at Alexandra Palace, as well as within single productions. And while productions might tour or be copied, long production runs in one theatre were rare. Even the most successful were usually measured in months rather than years.

Two things gave the industry a core and coherence in this artistic wild west. First the style and influence of the great actor-managers — the likes of Henry Irving, Charles Kean and Henry Beerbohm Tree in "legitimate" theatre; and of George Conquest and others in more populist performance. And second, the new theatres with their ever-more sophisticated stage technology.

At Alexandra Palace, it is the early pantomimes and spectacles, produced specifically for the theatre, or heavily adapted for it, that are the defining productions. Clearly the touring productions of plays and operas, which were the mainstay of the Victorian period at the Palace, used the stage machinery. But it is unlikely it was used in its full glory as a defining part of the production.

There were (as far is currently known) six Christmas pantomimes: The Yellow Dwarf (1875), St George and the Dragon (1877), Dick Whittington and his Cat (1878), Little Jack Horner (1879), Puss in Boots (1880) and Hop O' My Thumb (1881).

In addition there were three "summer" pantomimes (they only became exclusively associated with Christmas later): the first spectacle, Minerva, in May 1875, Turko the Terrible (Easter 1876) and The Triumph of Summer, described as a masque, in July 1880.

Little is known at the moment about The Triumph of Summer, or Dick Whittington. But the others reveal a mine of information about the theatre of the age and the kind of productions a large Victorian theatre built for spectacle and music would produce. Re-imaging the theatre of the period is, of course, greatly helped by the survival of the stage and the basic infrastructure of its machinery.

First of all, the cast lists and credits indicate that any continuities did not result from a resident company of actors — though the names of many actors and performers do recur. Where there are continuities, they appear in stage technicians and designers.

For instance, Mr Lightfoot (Victorian formalities not helpful here) is credited for "Appointments" on Minerva, and latterly for "Properties" on The Yellow Dwarf, St George, Triumph of Summer, Puss in Boots and Hop O' My Thumb. Mr Blanchard is credited for "Machinery" on St George, Triumph of Summer, Puss in Boots and Hop O' My Thumb.

It may be that they worked on other productions too, but we lack recorded credits. The only other person credited in these roles in the information we have so far is for a Mr Littlejohn for Machinery on The Yellow Dwarf.

Similarly, we have several credits for Mr and Mrs Stinchcombe for Costume or Dresses (St George, Triumph of Summer, Puss in Boots and Hop O' My Thumb). More importantly, Mr TH Friend is credited as producer/director for three productions (Little Jack Horner, Triumph of Summer and Puss in Boots), as well as a number of other productions.

Others with multiple credits include John Lauri for "Ballet" on St George, Little Jack Horner, Triumph of Summer and Puss in Boots. The Lauri family was a prominent theatrical family. The "Celebrated Lauri family" is credited with the Harlequinade in The Yellow Dwarf, with John as the Clown, Mr G (George) Lauri as Pantaloon and Madame Lauri as Columbine. George Lauri plays Harlequin and Jack O' Lantern later in Puss in Boots.

The most famous theatre family associated with the Palace is the

Conquests. George Conquest directed and played The Yellow Dwarf in the first Alexandra Palace pantomime, in which Miss Laura Conquest is credited as Little Great Britain. In a neat symmetry, George Conquest Jnr was producer and director of the last Victorian pantomime at the Palace, Hop O' My Thumb, also appearing as King No-body.

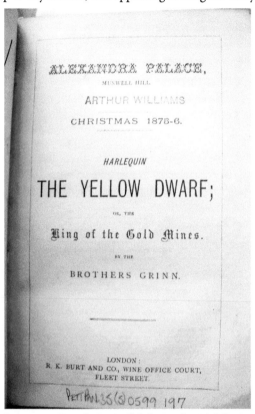

Yellow Dwarf title page — From the Pettingell Collection, Special Collections & Archives, Templeman Library, University of Kent, Canterbury, UK

Other family groups revealed by the production credits include the Espinosas: L (Leon) Espinosa, director of Minerva and ballet arranger for The Yellow Dwarf, and Madame Espinosa, one of the danseuses in Minerva; WH Payne and Fred Payne, King of Egypt and Dragon's son in St George; Aynsley Cooke, King Winter in Triumph of Summer and Aynsley Cooke Jnr, Goose in Puss In Boots; "The Great Little Rowella" (Charity Boy) and Dolph Rowella (Jack Pudding) in Triumph of Summer; and Reuben and Minnie Inch in Hop O' My Thumb.

The credits just provide a small window into such theatrical families. The pantomimes had 100 or more performers, and a large number of stage hands would be needed to work the stage. It's likely that many of these would have been related, all working on the same productions.

Another interesting feature of Victorian theatre is how the rapidly expanding sector offered opportunities to women in prominent, if not equal, roles to men, which were not available in most areas of life. Only in later Victorian days did Henry Irving turn acting into a "profession", but the popularity and prominence of the theatre allowed some female performers to achieve significant status and sometimes independent income and wealth. This was less often in creative positions. Only the choreographer Katti Lanner, the ballet arranger on Hop O' My Thumb, receives a significant creative credit in the Alexandra Palace pantomimes.

But as performers, whether dramatic actresses such as Sarah Siddons and Ellen Terry, or premiere danseuses, or opera singers; or in burlesque, music hall or pantomime, women could develop careers not possible in most other spheres. Letty Lind, who appeared as Princess Prettypet in Alexandra Palace's Puss in Boots, was later reckoned to be one of the highest-paid performers of her era.

There was an influx of women into the theatre after 1860 — which also meant an influx of children, given the family nature of the business. Occasionally we see named child performers, usually the offspring of leading actors. But in spectacular performances which depended on numbers, children could be a useful and cheap way of fleshing out the crowd scenes.

The V&A guide to Victorian Pantomime comments: "Christmas pantomimes often included children, and larger theatres such as Drury Lane and Covent Garden might include two children's ballets. The children who appeared in pantomime were mostly from working-class backgrounds. They were expected to work hard and to be extremely disciplined during rehearsals. When the show was running, they had a long evening's work — pantomimes starting at 7pm often didn't finish until midnight. It could be fun, however, and more importantly it meant earning a regular wage for a few weeks."

However, the introduction of compulsory education in 1874 put some curbs of this ready source of labour. In 1880, the Palace fell foul of the Tottenham School Board for the "employment of numerous children in theatrical performances at the palace in contravention of the Education Act 1870 and of the Board's bylaws".

According to Carrington: "Forty to 50 children were engaged in one performance alone, five-sixths of whom appeared to be under the age of 13, some 'scarcely fit to leave their mother's side.'"

He continues: "In one debate one speaker said, 'One young child appeared as Mr Gladstone, another as Lord Beaconsfield and a third as Napoleon Bonaparte. They should be learning to spell instead of being allowed to represent such exalted individuals, the doing of which would have the effect of puffing them up with such notions of their own superiority that they would come to the conclusion that they could do without education altogether.'"

Unfortunately, we have been unable to identify the production.

The Alexandra Palace pantomimes show all the major characteristics of the maturing form — from great spectacle and fantastic stories, to the characters, set-piece clowning, and celebrity turns — many of which survive today.

Perhaps the most prominent element which no longer exists is the Harlequinade, a sequence that harks right back to the origins of pantomime in the street theatre of Commedia dell'Arte. The Commedia originated in Italy in the 16th century and was spread around Europe by touring family groups who passed down their skills and costumes. It was a very physical form of theatre, including dance, music, tumbling and clowning.

While these elements survive in modern pantomimes, the stock characters and costumes have long gone. Originally the stock characters — the old man Pantalone, his artful servant Arlecchino and his amour Columbine, Pierrot the clown — had set gestures and costumes that reflected their characters, though the stories were often improvised and satirised current events or ideas.

After the Restoration in Britain in 1660 and the reopening of the theatres, Commedia characters starting appearing on the stage, with Arlecchino transformed into Harlequin, a quicksilver magical character, involved in energetic chases and acrobatics. The other main characters also continued — Pantalone becoming Pantaloon — except for Pulcinella, the coarse stupid servant. He would foster a separate tradition which stayed in the streets: the Punch and Judy show.

Entertainments developed around the Harlequinade were first called pantomimes in the early 18th century by John Rich, the actor-manager of the Theatre Royal, Drury Lane, and for the next century and a half, Harlequin and the Harlequinade remained a key part of the pantomime, usually leading up to the finale. The set format was a sequence of energetic chases, in which the star-crossed lovers Harlequin (in his chequered costume) and Columbine are kept apart by Pantaloon, Columbine's father, aided by the clown, while his servants play tricks on him.

The credits we have for the Alexandra Palace pantomimes seem to indicate variations on the characters and format. The Yellow Dwarf, for instance, has the four main characters, plus a Harlequina and adds other characters, such as Funny Policeman, and novelty acts, including performing dogs and skaters.

Two other traditions were linked to the Harlequinade, and in particular, the increasing use of scenery, of which one survives and one has now virtually disappeared — at least in pantomime.

John Rich choreographed the chase scenes through different locations — often local streets familiar to the audience — using collapsing pieces of scenery (usually hinged). Harlequin would use a wooden stick or paddle to hit the scenery to make the change — hence the term slapstick. This form of exaggerated physical and visual clowning is, of course, still a key part of modern pantomime (Oh, yes it is).

Two of the leading Victorian proponents of the Harlequinade appeared in the Palace's St George and the Dragon: WH Payne and his son Fred. William Henry Payne is credited with developing much of the action of the contemporary Harlequinade and was a master of comic mime. Fred became known for playing Harlequin and his brother Harry for playing the clown. Sadly, WH Payne died just less than a year after his performance at the Palace, in 1878, and Fred died age 39 two years later in 1880. (Harry continued his career, playing the clown for the last 12 years of his life at Drury Lane. The writer George Grossmith described him as "the best clown in my time".)

The Grand Transformation scene began as a way of segueing into the Harlequinade, first of all by simply removing pantomime headgear and costumes to reveal the Commedia costumes beneath. But as productions became bigger and scenery and stage technology more advanced, the whole stage went through an almost magical transformation using all the available tricks to effect a seamless change.

The Tottenham and Edmonton Weekly Herald describes the transformation scene in The Yellow Dwarf thus: "The transformation is a marvel of colour, brilliancy, and elegant form; and the use of a curtain of tinsel slips, on to which various coloured lights are directed is an effect as unique as it is charming."

The transformation scene disappeared with the Harlequinade in the

20th century, except for the changing of the pumpkin and mice into a coach and footmen in Cinderella, as the heroine becomes resplendent in ball gown. Modern pantomimes, with smaller budgets and mainly aimed at children, haven't the resources for such spectacle, but transformations can still be found in high-end musicals, using technical wizardry the Victorians could only marvel at.

Most of the other traditions of the Victorian pantomime still continue, albeit rejigged and tweaked, some of which reach back into the earliest days of pantomime.

The episodic nature of performance, with many scene changes (maybe not so many in today's straitened circumstances) and interludes of music, dancing and clowning, harks back to the influence of melodrama and burlesque in the early 19th century. This structure was used to circumvent the Licensing Act but also appealed to a growing working-class audience.

According to a V&A's guide to 19th Century Theatre, the first performance labelled a melodrama was Thomas Holcroft's A Tale of Mystery in 1802. It goes on to describe the genre:

"Melodrama consisted of short scenes interspersed with musical accompaniment and was characterised by simple morality, good and evil characters and overblown acting style. Characters in melodrama were stereotypical — there was always a villain, a wronged maiden and a hero. The emotions of the actors was played out in the music and accompanied by dramatic tableau. Because of these musical interludes a melodrama was not considered a 'play' and thus evaded the monopoly of the patent theatres.

"Early melodrama aimed to appeal to a working-class audience. Indeed the heroes and heroines were nearly always from the working class and the baddies were aristocrats or the local squire."

Pantomime was and remains a form of theatre largely aimed at a working-class audience and most of these characteristics continue. Characters often have names that reflect the qualities they are meant to represent — Princess Prettypet and Prince Perfect in Puss in Boots; Demon Ignorance and Fairy Commonsense in Little Jack Horner. In Mid-Victorian times many names were emblematic as well. The first scene of Yellow Dwarf has Jack Frost, Snowdrop, Jolly Christmas Time, Good Cheer and The Shortest Day.

Many pantomimes today still have the standard characters: a quick search picks up a production at the Theatre Royal Windsor with an absolutely traditional cast of Aladdin, the evil Abanazar, the Genie of the Lamp (played by a not-so traditional Basil Brush, an interesting variation on the long tradition of animal performers), the Empress, Princess Jasmine, Wishee Washee and Widow Twankey.

But others have almost completely updated characters. Paignton's 2013-14 production of Sleeping Beauty has Nurse Dottie Dettol and Bad Witch Hazel, Princess Rose and King Cactus (obviously a prickly customer), and three supporting characters called Muddles, Fetch and Carrie

Similarly, the hero-villain-thwarted love theme is still pretty much universal, and although pantomimes from Victorian times onwards, based on fairy and folk tales, are full of kings, queens, princes, princesses, grand viziers etc, usually the hero is an underdog (Cinderella, Dick Whittington, Aladdin). And the baddies are usually stuck-up (Ugly Sisters) or power-crazed (Abanazar).

There is, of course, one tradition particular to pantomime: cross dressing. This has a long tradition because in Elizabethan theatre women couldn't appear on the stage, so women's parts had to be played by men. Women were free to appear on the stage after the Restoration, but the tradition for women to take male roles seems to have originated in ballet at the end of the 18th century. With the increasing popularity of the ballerina, many female dancers took the male roles.

So-called breeches parts in drama seem to have developed in the early part of the 19th century in burlesque acts. Madame Vestris was the first major female actor-manager, running the Olympic Theatre in London from 1830-49. Her appearance in burlesques in short trousers and tights made her a sex symbol of the age. By the 1880s the lead male character in pantomime was almost always played by a women — the principal boy. Principal boys at Alexandra Palace include Suzie Vaughan as St George and Caroline Parkes as Puss in Boots.

Pantomime dames began to appear at the same time, notably the clown Joseph Grimaldi, playing the Baron's wife in Cinderella in 1820. By the late 19th century, music hall stars were taking the roles — most famously Marie Lloyd, and Dan Leno, who was first asked to play the Dame in Jack and the Beanstalk in 1886 by George Conquest Jnr, then the manager of the Surrey Theatre. But Herbert Campbell, who appeared as King Marmalade in The Yellow Dwarf at Alexandra Palace, also became a famous dame. Dames at Alexandra Palace include Sam Wilkinson as Dame Noodle in Hop O' My Thumb.

The pantomimes at Alexandra Palace, like the stage on which they were dependent, were produced at a period of transition. They were mounted with state-of-the-art stage technology and production techniques, but there is much that seems still rooted in in the Harlequinade and burlesque traditions of spectacle and clowning. Even the exaggerated titles looked back. Not as extreme as some maybe (Harlequin and the Tyrant of Gobblemupandshrunkemdowno), but the full titles — Harlequin The Yellow Dwarf or The King of the Gold Mines; Hop O' My Thumb or Harlequin No-body, Some-body, Busy-body , and the Wicked Ogre with the Seven-League Boots — hardly have the direct impact or resonance of Cinderella or Aladdin.

The change that was shaping the late Victorian pantomime — and essentially the form as it is today — was the development of new pantomime stories. The Harlequinade pantomimes were degenerating into absurdity by the 1840s. But the end of the Licensing Act meant that previously non-licensed theatres could now perform plays with a proper narrative.

Two writers in particular rejuvenated the stock of pantomime tales. The burlesque specialist HJ Byron and theatre manager and writer JR Planche introduced new stories, giving pantomime more narrative structure and introducing wordplay and punning as key elements. Both were prolific, Planche penning over 170 plays of various kinds and Byron about 150.

Planche translated and adapted French fairy tales from 17th-century France, often based on even older folk tales, turning them into theatrical extravaganzas . Madame d'Aulnoy (1650-1705) is said to have coined the term fairy tales and originated stories such as Cunning Cinders, a version of Cinderella, Goldilocks and the Three Bears, and The Yellow Dwarf. From Charles Perrault (1628-1703) came Puss in Boots, another version of Cinderella, Little Red Riding Hood, Mother Goose and Sleeping Beauty.

Victorian writers then turned to English folk tales or nursery rhymes — Dick Whittington, Babes In The Wood, St George, Little Goody Two Shoes; and the Arabian Nights — Ali Baba and the Forty Thieves, Sinbad the Sailor and Aladdin. HJ Byron's pantomimes included Jack the Giant Killer, King Arthur, and Aladdin. The Brothers Grinn — Edward L Blanchard (1820-89) and Thomas Longdon Greenwood (1806-79) — who wrote Alexandra Palace's Yellow Dwarf, also wrote pantomime versions of Sinbad, Bluebeard and Cinderella.

It's worth looking in some detail at how the Palace's pantomimes interpreted and embodied this history, as they are the keynote production of the Alexanda Palace Theatre.

Pantomimes and spectacles 1875-76

Minerva, Yellow Dwarf, Turko the Terrible

The first spectacle and two pantomimes at the Alexandra Palace Theatre, before the first financial crisis hit the second Palace, can perhaps be seen as representing the height of the Theatre's ambitions to use its state of the art stage and equipment to full effect, with no expense spared. The two spring productions (Minerva and Turko the Terrible) would seem to indicate a desire to exploit the potential of the stage all year round, while The Yellow Dwarf, which we look at in some detail, perhaps exemplifies the artistic — or at least technical — ambitions of the Theatre.

Minerva

Whit Monday, 17 May 1875
New Grand Spectacle
Minerva: The Tutelary Goddess of the Arts and Sciences

Director	L Espinosa
Music composer	J Hamilton Clarke
New scenery	T Grieve and Son
Costume design	M Faustin
Costumes	S May & Co
Wigs	Mr Clarkson
Machinery	Mr Littlejohn
Appointments	Mr Lightfoot
Lime light	Mr Cox, gas engineer
Premiere danseuse	Virginia Milani, from Scala Milan
	Madame and Monsieur L Espinosa

Whit Monday, 17 May 1875, was the first big day for the rebuilt Palace, which had opened for the first time on 1 May. Billed as a Great

National Holiday Festival, the Weekly Herald reported that 94,125 people had passed through the turnstiles to enjoy a "host of amusements", including two performances in the theatre.

The first was a performance at 12.30 consisting of an operetta by Louis Diehl, The Elfin Tree, followed by Minerva; and an evening performance starting at 17.30 of a farce by William Brough and Andrew Halliday, The Area Belle, followed by Minerva.

Minerva is described as a new grand spectacle in three tableaux. It seems designed both to demonstrate the high-minded aspirations of the Palace and show off its state of the art stage and machinery to best effect. Minerva is described as descending from heaven to create the arts and sciences, with "the transition from barbarism to civilisation effected before our very eyes".

The scale of the production is hinted at by the number of characters and the presence of a corps de ballet of 150.

The tableaux take place in ancient Greece and mix "Historic Personages": Homer (Poetry); Phidias (Sculpture); Raphael (Painting); Hippocrates (Medicine); Archimedes (Geometry); Galileo (Astronomy); Newton (Mathematics); Shakespeare (Drama); Milton (Poetry); Wren (Architecture); Fulton (Mechanics); and Watt (Engineering). And "Mythological personages": Jupiter; Juno; Pluto; Ceres; Vulcan; Venus; Mercury; Diana; Neptune; Rhea; Apollo; Flora; Saturnus; Pales; Pomona; and Vertumnus.

Tableau 1 consists of four parts: The Repose of Olympus, The Twelve Hours, The Chimes, (Madame Espinosa and Corps de Ballet); The Apparition of the Goddess Minerva (Mdlle Virginia Milani); The creation of the arts and sciences; and the Grand Allegorical Personification from Paganism to Modern Times.

Tableau 2 presents Minerva on Earth (Mdlle Virginia Milani); The Ploughers; The Reapers; The Thrashers; The Harvesters; The Vintagers.

Tableau 3 offers The Temple of Jupiter; Apparition to Raphael (Miss L Charlton); Phidias and his apprentices (Messrs Knight, Fish, Kimberley, Ives); Allegorical subjects represented by groups — History (Clio), Astronomy (Urania), Music (Euterpe), Fame (Calliope); Mala Rassiskala — Character Dance (Madame and Mons L Espinosa); The Cyclops; The Tritonian Dances (Mdlle Milani, Mme Espinosa, Corps de Ballet); La Peltata (Mdlles Richard and St Leger); Grand Pyrrhic & Saturnalian Dances (Mdlle Milani, Madame Espinosa, 150 Corps de Ballet).

The Tottenham and Edmonton Weekly Herald reported that both

performances "were witnessed by large and enthusiastic audiences, who loudly applauded some of the tableaux, and went into ecstasies at the dancing of Madlle Milani".

The creative team was a distinguished one, with extensive West End experience. The director was almost certainly Leon Espinosa, born 1825, who was one of the most renowned dancers of the day, having worked both at the Paris Opera and in Moscow. He moved to London in 1872 and worked on productions at Covent Garden and worldwide.

The young composer and probably conductor, James Hamilton Clarke (b 1840), succeeded Arthur Sullivan as the organist of St Peter's South Kensington, leaving soon after to become a theatre conductor, and was later to become musical director for Gilbert and Sullivan. Before Minerva he had been Richard D'Oyly Carte's musical director and then worked at the Opera Comique and Theatre Royal.

Grieve and Son were noted scene painters and a draw for audiences by themselves. Thomas Grieve's father had been a noted scene painter as had his brother William. Thomas worked from 1862 with his son Thomas Walford Grieve, who is credited with designing the stage at Alexandra Palace. The Grieve Family archive of 655 scene paintings is held at London's Senate House — they were bought from a junk shop in 1939 and donated to the library in 1943.

The Monsieur Faustin credited for the costume design is possibly the French artist Faustin Betbeder known for his caricatures of public figures — including a famous one of Darwin as a monkey — who moved to London after the Franco-Prussian war and is recorded as having done costume designs around this time.

Perhaps we should also remember Mr Cox, the gas engineer, credited with Limelight, suggesting the importance of the lighting in this spectacle, which was all about the sets and costumes, music and dance, rather than any dramatic qualities.

The Yellow Dwarf

Christmas 1875-January 1876
Harlequin the Yellow Dwarf or the King of the Gold Mines

Story	Brothers Grinn
Director	George Conquest
Music composed/arranged	Oscar H Barrett
Scenery	Wm Brew, Mr Soames, J Johnstone, Henri Nedme

Comic scenes arranged	J Lauri
Ballet arranged	M. Espinosa
Properties	Mr Lightfoot
Dresses	Auguste et Cie, Paris
Machinery	Mr Littlejohn

The Yellow Dwarf is the first production with all systems go, using all the bells and whistles (almost literally: whistles were used by stage hands to indicate a scene change — which is why whistling in the theatre is bad luck. It could result in shifting people or scenery at the wrong time, causing injury). The Yellow Dwarf adds drama and human action to pure spectacle and was masterminded by one of the great pantomimists of the day, George Conquest.

However, the fact that individual scenes are credited to different people, indicates that the mise en scene was still at the forefront of the production.

Scene 1: Silver Hall of Icicles in Jack Frost's Winter Palace

Scene by	Henri Nedme, J Johnstone
Jack Frost	Mr Fredericks
Snowdrop	Miss Alma Edrof
Jolly Christmas Time	Mr Stone
Good Cheer	Miss Inch
The Shortest Day	Miss K Smith

The character Jolly Christmas Time suggests a pantomime should be created; and Good Cheer offers to find a storyline.

Scene 2: The Golden Temples of India's Fairyland

Scene by	Wm Brew, Henri Nedme
Little Great Britain	Miss Laura Conquest
Union Jacks	Misses Jean and E Barry

The search for the storyline takes the characters to India's "Fairyland" and the scene ends with a Grand Ballet.

Scene 3: The Orange Grove and Withered Tree (Moonlight)

| Scene by | J Johnstone |

Meliodorus, King of the Gold Mines	Miss Carry Nelson
Tiny Tim (his tiger)	Miss Lizzie Claremont
Zaffron, the Yellow Dwarf	George Conquest
Okur and Tawnee	Jackley Brothers
Princess Allfair	Miss Dot Robins
Foresters	Misses Barnet and Dolman
Black Slaves	Hob, Nob, Bob, Rob

Princess Allfair plucks an orange from a tree. The Yellow Dwarf, disguised at first as a tree and then as an owl (all played by George Conquest), proposes marriage to the Princess, as a punishment for taking the fruit. (The names indicate racial stereotyping that would be unacceptable today.)

Scene 4: The Grand Reception Hall in King Marmalade's Palace

Scene by	William Brew, Henri Nedme
King Marmalade	Herbert Campbell
Candi (Chamberlain)	Fred Hughes

The Princess and the Yellow Dwarf (now in human form) are with King Marmalade, the Princess's father. King Meliodorus, the King of the Gold Mines, arrives and asks King Marmalade if he can marry the Princess. The Desert Fairy says King Meliodorus cannot marry the Princess, because she is engaged to marry the Yellow Dwarf.

Scene 5: Outside the Steel Castle of the Yellow Dwarf

Scene by	J Johnstone
Desert Fairy	Miss A Forrest
Magnet	Mr G Conquest jnr

King Meliodorus and the Desert Fairy have tracked the Yellow Dwarf to the castle. To find the Yellow Dwarf the Desert Fairy enlists the help of Magnet, one of her Sprites.

Scene 6: Cobweb Caves and Spider's Glen

Scene by	Wm Brew, Henri Nedme

Magnet (played by George Conquest Junior) chases the Yellow Dwarf.

Scene 7: Room in King Marmalade's Palace

Scene by	J Johnstone

King Meliodorus tells King Marmalade that the Yellow Dwarf will trouble them no more.

Scene 8: The Glowworm Glade in the Fern Forest

The Grand Transformation and the Grand Finale.

Scenes by	Mr Soames, J Johnstone

Harlequinade by	Celebrated Lauri family
Clown	John Lauri
Pantaloon	Mr G Lauri
Harlequin	Mr Sims
Columbine	Madame Lauri
Harlequina	Miss C White
Funny policeman	Mr WH Ash
Performing dogs/goats	Nat Emmett
Great skaters	Brothers Guida
African miniature man	Adonis

Scene 1	Toy Mart: Twist, Tobacconist; Pekoe, Grocer
Scene 2	Suburban quiet lodgings
Scene 3	Shadow pantomime
Scene 4	Realms of bliss

Grand finale

Adding energetic action to spectacle also brought risks: the Weekly Herald reported: "The Grand Christmas Pantomime was to have been produced on Tuesday last, but owing to the illness of Mr G Conquest, who has twisted his spine and sprained the muscles of his back, it had to be postponed for a few days."

So the exact dates it was performed are not known (probably at least until 22 January), but it appears to have been a success. The Alexandra Palace Programme of Arrangements for 1876-77 comments that the pantomime was written expressly for Alexandra Palace by the Brothers Grinn and that "it was produced at great cost, and pronounced to be among the first successes of the Season".

It added: "It would have continued for a longer period had not other pressing arrangements, requiring the use of the Theatre, compelled the Directors to withdraw it." (Such pressing arrangements would not, unfortunately, last for long and the Palace was in dire financial problems before the year was out.)

Cobweb Caves and Spider's Glen, The Yellow Dwarf — From the Pettingell Collection, Special Collections & Archives, Templeman Library, University of Kent, Canterbury, UK

Once again there was a creative team of considerable experience and this time a cast of some note.

The Brothers Grinn were the duo Edward Blanchard and Thomas Greenwood. Blanchard was one of the great jobbing writers of the Victorian age who began writing as a teenager to support himself after his father died. He had written 30 plays by the time he was 20, paid as little as £2 a play, and supplemented his earnings by writing advertisements, comic songs and journalism. Among other publications, he wrote for and edited several periodicals, including Punch, and became drama critic of the Daily Telegraph.

He was hired to write regularly for the Olympic Theatre in 1841 and also wrote for the Surrey Theatre, but he was most successful as a writer for the Drury Lane pantomimes, which he contributed to for 37 years. In 1891, a two-volume memoir of his experiences was published, described as "a memorial of arduous and incessant struggles, and, until near the end, of miserable pay", but also "a delightful picture of one of the kindest, most genial and lovable of Bohemians".

The Yellow Dwarf was originally produced at Drury Lane, but whether and how much the Alexandra Palace version was based on that, is not known. Or indeed how much input there was from the director, George Conquest, himself a pantomime writer.

The Conquest family — George's sons, George Jnr, Fred and Arthur, all followed in his footsteps — was one of the great theatrical families of the era and perhaps the leading family in pantomime. George Augustus Oliver — Conquest was a stage name — made his first theatrical appearance, according to the Dictionary of National Biography, in 1837, the year of his birth, as a child-in-arms in a farce at the Garrick Theatre, where his father was the manager.

He made several appearances there as a child, before being educated in Boulogne, where he was a contemporary of the leading French actor, Benoit Coquelin. His fluency in French stood him well as a writer. He wrote more than 100 plays, many of them adapted from French originals. Like Blanchard, he started young. His first plays were adapted from the French, while he was still at school, for his father, who had become manager of the Grecian Theatre in City Road in 1851.

His first play, Woman's Secret, or Richlieu's Wager, was produced at the Grecian in 1853 and he was highly successful on stage in 1855, as the Artful Dodger in an adaptation of Oliver Twist. That year he fulfilled his career ambition for the first time, when he appeared as an acrobatic pantomimist in his own pantomime, Harlequin Sun, Moon and the Seven Sisters. He adapted and appeared in many plays at the Grecian, and became manager of the theatre on his father's death in 1872.

In all, he produced 45 pantomimes and performed in an estimated 27. He is credited with inventing the modern method of "flying" using "invisible" wires, used to such great effect in The Yellow Dwarf. But such stage acrobatics — flying across the stage, appearing and disappearing through traps in the stage, jumping through "mirrors" — was a hazardous business, as the delay in the opening of Yellow Dwarf suggests. In one production, The Devil on Two Sticks, he used 29 traps — one vampire trap and 28 other traps.

He claimed that he had broken every bone in his body. His most serious accident happened in New York in 1880, during a performance of The Grim Goblin at Wallacks Theatre, when trapeze ropes broke. There was some suspicion of sabotage by a rival — yet another hazard of the times, perhaps.

Despite his long, active career — he retired from performance in 1894 — he only appeared on a couple of occasions in the West End. Throughout this period there was an extensive theatre industry in the East End, of which now little remains. He died in 1901, leaving a fortune of £64,000, probably in excess of £5m today.

His impact on stage cannot be doubted — despite a speech

impediment offstage, which disappeared when he acted. The North Middlesex Chronicle report of the Yellow Dwarf said that he was "the life and soul of everything in which he is engaged. His leaps are of the most surprising character; while his dive of some 30ft to somewhere or other — we don't know where — is a miraculous feat".

The composer and arranger on The Yellow Dwarf, Oscar Barrett, although little known today, also has a noted place in Victorian pantomime. Starting at Crystal Palace in south London before moving to the West End, he composed music for Drury Lane productions and with several key writers. His songs include Roses & Diamonds with EL Blanchard, and Nonsense! Yes!! By Jove!!! with Harry Nicholls, who was later part of a famous double act with Herbert Campbell.

He went on to produce his own pantomimes, mainly at the Lyceum Theatre. He reportedly claimed in 1894 to have arranged and produced 47 "fairy extravaganzas" or pantomimes. Professor Jeffrey Richards accords him a particular status as the last great proponent of a kind of pantomime untainted by the music hall and variety acts introduced by Augustus Harris at Drury Lane.

"In the 1880s and 1890s he [Harris] was seriously challenged by the now forgotten Oscar Barrett who first at Crystal Palace and later in the West End staged delicate and elegant Christmas shows of the old kind. His Cinderella at the Lyceum was hailed by some critics as a perfect example of the genre.

"But Barrett lost the battle and retired to the provinces. The Harris formula, complete with music hall element, carried on triumphantly into the 20th century to provide the blueprint for the pantomimes of today, where music hall stars have been replaced by soap stars, reality TV personalities, retired politicians and faded Hollywood stars."

One interesting characteristic of the Palace's Yellow Dwarf is that there are different people credited with the design of each scene — perhaps an indication of the money lavished on this production; but little is known about those involved — William Brew, Henri Nedme, and the even more anonymous J Johnstone and Mr Soames.

On stage, beside the Conquests and the other theatre family the Lauris (responsible for the Harlequinade), the notable performers are Herbert Campbell (King Marmalade) and the principal boy, Carry Nelson (Meliodorus).

Campbell's career began in less than illustrious fashion as part of a "black-face" minstrel act in the 1860s, before he became a comic vocalist in East End music halls, with ditties such as Did You Ever Hear a Girl

Say No? and They Were a Lovely Pair. He made his debut in pantomime at the Theatre Royal Liverpool in 1871, and was later hired to appear in Christmas pantomime at the Grecian Theatre in London by George Conquest, to repeat one of his roles.

MR. GEORGE CONQUEST AS THE YELLOW DWARF.
MISS DOT ROBINS AS PRINCESS ALLFAIR.

Princess Allfair and the Yellow Dwarf — From the Pettingell Collection, Special Collections & Archives, Templeman Library, University of Kent, Canterbury, UK

Campbell would certainly have made his presence felt at Alexandra Palace: he was over six feet tall and weighed about 250lbs. The writer Max Beerbohm described him as "the offspring of some mystical union between beef and thunder". From 1882 he appeared in a series of pantomimes at Drury Lane, lasting until his death in 1904. From 1888 he appeared with the diminutive music hall star Dan Leno, which was highly successful but which many critics, such as EL Blanchard, thought corrupted the pantomime format.

Carry Nelson appears to be an Australian actress who came to Britain around the 1860s. The Melbourne Argus reported in 1882: "Miss Carry Nelson left the colony a bright and clever girl, full of promise, but with undeveloped powers. She returns to it with that promise more than fulfilled and with her splendid gifts of voice, personal attractions, and histrionic ability ripened into maturity."

The review in the Weekly Herald of 1 January 1876 gives an idea of how The Yellow Dwarf appeared to the contemporary audience: "After the overture — in which the introduction of Der Freischutz is ignobly mixed up with popular strains — we find ourselves before the Silver Hall of Icicles in Jack Frost's Winter Palace. Here Jack is holding court, attended by his faithful Snowballs, and visited by Jolly Time, Snowdrop, Shortest Day, and Good Cheer.

"After touching on the topics of the day (and revealing a clever picture of the Arctic expedition in its winter quarters), Jack Frost casts about for a new sensation, and, after showing his various games, such as cricket, trap, bat-and-ball, shuttle-cock and battle-dore, dominoes, and cards, Jolly Time suggests a pantomime, of which Good Cheer promises to find the plot, Jack Frost having to supply the rime.

"The scene now changes to the Golden Temples of India's Fairyland, where Little Britain exercises sovereign sway. This tiny monarch bids The Yellow Dwarf to come, meanwhile celebrating the visit of Christmas Time, Jack Frost, and Good Cheer with a ballet of Bright Fancies. The tableau here presented is one of exceeding beauty, and the evolutions of the coryphees are graceful and well designed. The streamers used, as in the maypole dance, are, however, too pronounced in colour, completely killing all their surroundings. With this exception the harmony of the picture is perfect, and the spectacle one of rare charm.

"The action proper of the opening now begins in the Orange Grove, where stands the Withered Tree. Travelling in the neighbourhood are Meliodorus, King of the Goldmines, with his retinue, and the Princess Allfair (Toutebelle) with her suite. The Princess Allfair, who compels implicit obedience from her retainers, commands them to pluck her an orange from a certain tree which is evidently beneath the guardianship of some very awkward looking red lions. The courage of the servants, however, fails them, and the Princess herself picks the coveted fruit.

"Now there suddenly appears upon the scene a withered old Tree — as ordinary a gnarled old stump as ever was chopped up for firewood, apparently — but to the wonder and astonishment not only of the Princess, but of the spectators, the tree begins to develop human features, and something of human nature also, for it deliberately winks at Princess Allfair. Next it speaks, then thrusts out its roots and begins to stalk about in the most unconcerned way 'as to the manner born'.

"The Tree asks the Princess to be his wife, and gives her five minutes for reflection — the allotted time being appropriately devoted to singing and dancing by the young lady. When the Tree reappears at the expiration of the five minutes, it speedily undergoes another metamorphosis, the trunk and limbs vanishing, and leaving in their stead a preternaturally sapient little Owl, whose big eyes glare with the fierceness of a policeman's bull's-eye, and (we say reproachfully) are only too well adapted for the furious winking in which the bird of wisdom indulges.

"But, wonder upon wonders, when the princess makes a very natural objection to the propriety of marrying a bird, the Owl straightway disappears, and [she] discovers an ugly little Yellow Dwarf, who demands her hand as the penalty for stealing the orange. His lions and sprites come at his call, and bear the princess away.

"In the next scene, which is in the Grand Reception Hall, in King Marmalade's Palace, we find everybody, and especially Candi, the Lord Chamberlain, in grief for the loss of the Princess. The Yellow Dwarf has, however, spirited her back to her father's palace, and now comes to give her his greeting. At the wish of Princess Allfair, Zaffron ceases to be a dwarf, and regains his human form.

"Here occurs some good comic business between King Marmalade and Zaffron. The King of the Gold Mines enters, with all his gorgeous train, to ask the hand of the Princess, but Zaffron intervenes, and despite all opposition carries her off to his Steel Castle. Here he is followed by Meliodorus, to whose assistance Magnet is brought by the Desert Fairy, Magnet alone having the power to subdue the Yellow Dwarf.

"Accordingly they track Zaffron to the Cowbeb Caves and Spiders Glen, where an extraordinary chase commences. Zaffron sinks through the earth on beholding Magnet, and a second afterwards is seen flying through the air, at a giddy height. Nor is Magnet less agile, the two seeming to be here, there, and everywhere; vanishing from sight when least expected, and reappearing in the most unlikely localities.

"This 'Phantom Fight' is a thing to be seen, not to be described. The dwarf is caught, and here the opening virtually ends, though there is another front scene before the transformation — The Glowworm Glade in the Fern Forest, leading to the Desert Fairy's Floral Home — is reached. The transformation is a marvel of colour, brilliancy, and elegant form; and the use of a curtain of tinsel slips, on to which various coloured lights are directed is an effect as unique as it is charming."

The Herald's assessment is of an almost untrammelled success: "The fine proportions of the stage of the Alexandra Palace Opera Theatre lend themselves readily to the arrangement of those sheeny spectacles and attractive tableaux vivants, without which modern pantomime would be divested of one of its greatest charms; while the ample space at the disposal of the ballet master gives him full power to devise elaborate movements, groupings, &c., and to take advantage of the effective contrast of colour."

"There seems to be some little need of compression in the action, and much of the music might be omitted with advantage. But for splendour of appointments and novelty of effect, the Alexandra Palace pantomime cannot be surpassed."

If the aim was to create a Drury Lane in leafy north London, the Alexandra Palace Theatre seemed to be off to a flying start.

Turko the Terrible or the Great Princess Show

Easter 1876

Story by	William Brough
Producer	Mr Kilpack
Ballet	M Espinosa
Gambols	Fred Evans and troupe
Buonocore, King of the Golden Land	Hy. Moxon
Lord Kootoo, High Chamberlain	Mr G Peyton
Prince Amabel	Miss Edith Blande
Count Muffio	Miss Ida Hertz
Count Spoonio	Miss May Burney
Fairy Roseatinta	Miss Langley
Turko the Terrible	John Rouse (permission of Mrs Liston)
Gruffangrimio	Herbert Campbell
Meelimug	Fred Evans
Kutstic	Mr Franks
Violet, Turko's daughter	Miss Kate Vaughan
Tartarella	Miss Bella Cuthbert
Dragonetta	Miss Everard

Turko the Terrible was adapted from a burlesque called Prince Amabel by the writer William Brough staged at the Royalty Theatre in 1865. It seems Brough first turned it into a pantomime called Turko

TURKO THE TERRIBLE;

OR, THE

GREAT PRINCESS SHOW.

CHARACTERS.

BUONOCORE (King of the Golden Land—a beneficent Monarch, reigning in his people's love—in fact, the King of Hearts, and, as such, a regular trump; his unexceptionable rule proving the fallacy of the notion that there is no rule without exception) ....Mr. Hy. Moxon.

LORD KOOTOO (High Chamberlain at the Court of Buonocore; an official who, in this happy-going country, is much oftener found sitting in easy chairs than standing upon forms) .... Mr. G. Peyton.

PRINCE AMABEL (King Buonocore's Son and Heir)—a youth diminutive in stature, though great in *sighs*, a victim to "Love's young dream," which he is unable to *read aright*, and can only *sigh for*, receiving a lot of roses to make amends for his *lack o' daises*...Miss Edith Blande.

COUNT MUFFIO } (Friends of the Prince, accompanying } Miss Ida Hertz.
COUNT SPOONIO } him in his travels—a long walk, } Miss May Burney.
              which, it is hoped, may result in
              a long run) ....

THE FAIRY ROSEATINTA (the Good Genius of Prince Amabel and the Princess Violet) .... Miss Langley.

TURKO, CALLED THE TERRIBLE (King of the Iron Mountains—a very bad sovereign of the Author's own making, but which he hopes may *pass*, the inherent baseness of the metal being so thickly covered with *g(u)ilt*) ....Mr. John Rouse.
                        By permission of Mrs. Liston.

GRUFFANGRIMIO (his Prime Minister, a villain of the deepest die—in fact, a *dire* villain) ....Mr. Herbert Campbell.

MEELIMUG (an Officer of King Turko's Household—a very bad character, morally considered, and dramatically not a very good one)
                        Mr. Fred. Evans.

KUTSTIC ....(Captain of the Guard)....................Mr. Franks.

VIOLET (King Turko's youngest daughter, gifted by the Fairy Roseatinta with one charm, and, by nature, with no end of others) Miss Kate Vaughan.

TARTARELLA } (Daughters of King Turko by a former } Miss Bella Cuthbert.
            marriage—spinsters who, living at the
            unknown period of the Drama, may be
            called of an *uncertain age*, and who,
DRAGONETTA } though proud of their high rank, are } Miss Everard.
            quite ready to change their condition) /

Turko the Terrible cast list — From the Pettingell Collection, Special Collections &
Archives, Templeman Library, University of Kent, Canterbury, UK

the Terrible or The Fairy Roses in 1868. This in turn was adapted into a pantomime called Turko the Terrible by the Irish writer Edwin Hamilton for the Gaiety Theatre in Dublin for Christmas 1873.

This version was updated and revived many times in the following decades and became so much a part of Irish culture that it makes an appearance in the pages of James Joyce's Ulysses.

It's not clear what version was the basis for the Alexandra Palace production. Nothing is currently known about the producer, Mr Kilpack, but the Irish name suggests a possible a link to Hamilton's version of the pantomime.

William Brough's life was not without drama. His publican-turned-writer father was briefly kidnapped by Chartists in 1839 and was a prosecution witness in the trial of the Chartist leader John Frost, who was deported. As a result the family was ostracised and had to move to Manchester. Brough was apprenticed as a printer before trying his hand at journalism with his better known brother Robert.

He wrote mainly burlesques, including a version of Pygmalion for the Royalty theatre, and also worked with another writer, Andrew Halliday. The Brough brothers, along with Halliday, were founding members of the Savage Club, whose members down the years have included Wilkie Collins, Henry Irving, King Edward VII and Charlie Chaplin.

The Espinosas continued to provide the dance element, while Fred Evans and his troupe were the comic relief. The Evans were a family of music hall and circus performers. The most famous member was either the son or grandson of the Fred Evans credited here, who was born in 1889 and was a childhood friend of Charlie Chaplin, before becoming a silent film comedian, appearing in more than 200 short films as the character Pimple … many of which may have been shown at Alexandra Palace in the early years of the 20th century.

Perhaps the most interesting member of the cast was Kate Vaughan, now remembered mostly as a dancer and in particular as the originator of the "skirt dance".

According to the Dictionary of National Biography, she received "preliminary training in the dancing academy conducted by old Mrs Conquest" at the Grecian Theatre — perhaps George Conquest's mother? — before taking finishing lessons with ballet master John D'Auban. She first appeared on stage in music hall in 1870 as one of the Sisters Vaughan, a dance act with her sister Susie, who would appear at Alexandra Palace as St George in the Christmas 1877 pantomime.

In 1873 she is said to have originated the skirt dance after performing it in Dance of the Furies at the Holborn Theatre, repeating the act in Offenbach's Orpheus in the Underworld. The dance is described as a form of dance in which "women dancers would manipulate long, layered skirts with their arms to create a motion of flowing fabric. This was often in a darkened theatre with coloured projectors highlighting the patterns of their skirts."

D'Auban worked with Vaughan and taught the dance to many other artistes. The dance became popular at the Gaiety Theatre, and was a stock in trade of its chorus line, the Gaiety Girls. Other leading performers of the day, including Letty Lind also adopted the dance. It is reported that up to 100 yards of fabric could be used in the making of the dresses. Vaughan was associated with the Gaiety Theatre for seven years, but in the mid-1880s gave up dancing for health reasons and made a career in comedy, including a spell managing the Opera Comique. But it was for her dancing that she proved most successful with audiences.

The Dictionary of National Biography concludes: "In point of grace, magnetism and spirituality, Kate Vaughan was the greatest English dancer of her century. She owed little to early training and much to refinement and exquisite sense of rhythm."

With as yet no contemporary report or review of Turko, it's not known if she performed the dance at Alexandra Palace. But a similar use of light was noted in The Yellow Dwarf.

Otherwise the cast seems to be a little less illustrious than for The Yellow Dwarf, apart from Herbert Campbell. Carrington says there were 100 performers — again less grand than for Yellow Dwarf. It may be that the Palace's hope with this Easter production was to be able to produce pantomimes at Christmas, Easter and a spectacle in August. If so, financial reality was just about to intrude.

Pantomimes and spectacles 1877-82

St George and the Dragon, Dick Whittington and his Cat, Little Jack Horner, The Triumph of Summer, Puss in Boots, Hop O' My Thumb

St George and the Dragon or Harlequin the Seven Champions of Christendom

Christmas 1877

Story by	Brothers Grinn
Director/scenery	Henry Emden
Music (composer/conductor)	Frank Musgrave
Stage manager	TH Friend
Ballet	John Lauri
Dresses	Mr & Mrs Stinchcombe
Machinery	Mr Blanchard
Properties	Mr Lightfoot
St George	Susie Vaughan
King of Egypt	WH Payne
Dragon's Son/Harlequin	Fred Payne
Zazel	John Lauri (with the stage traps)
Princess Sabra	Miss Linda Verner
Grand Chamberlain	WB Fair
St Denis	Miss Lilla Howard
St Patrick	Miss Florence Chalgrove
St David	Miss Verdoni
St Andrew	Miss Clara Fisher
St Anthony	Miss L Bronte
St James	Miss Lillie Graham

Kalyba, The Enchantress	Miss Isabel Lewis
Premiere danseuse	Mdlle Luna
Pantaloon	Tully Louis
Columbine	Miss L Percival
Harlequina	Miss C Fisher
Clown	Harry Payne

In October 1876, the Palace closed after the Alexandra Palace Company sought a winding up order as its losses mounted. The Palace reopened in May 1877 under new management — Messrs Bertram and Roberts, who were the previous catering managers. Apart from the August Bank Holiday, events appear to be limited, so the pantomime was perhaps an attempt to restore the original aspirations of the Palace.

What we know of St George at present comes from the advertisements for the show in an Alexandra Palace daily programme of events and the local paper. The advert in the Weekly Herald promises: "The Christmas arrangements at this now permanently established place of amusement are unusually extensive. The piece de resistance will be a very elaborate pantomime, written by the Brothers Grinn."

The advert notes the importance of "trusting the general superintendence to an artist" — the scenery painter Henry Emden, of whom little is known except that he worked at Drury Lane (one of his scenes is in the V&A).

The stage manager on this production, TH Friend, was to become the producer-director of at least three of the next four pantomimes (information on Dick Whittington is currently not available). Information on Friend is equally scarce, though he seems to have been associated with a number of regional theatres, including in Brighton and Bristol. Even so, according to the advert, his name was "a guarantee that great spectacular effect and rollicking music and fun will abound".

The other new names on the production side are John Lauri, "well-known in connection with his productions at the Alhambra Theatre", who took over ballet production duties from Monsieur Espinosa and would do so for several of the remaining Palace pantomimes. The same is true of the costume designers, Mr and Mrs Stinchcome — presumably from the Drury Lane firm of theatrical costumiers.

The music was composed, arranged and conducted by Frank Musgrave, now a largely forgotten figure. Philip L Scowcroft, author of British Light Music Composers, calls him "an interesting figure, even if none of his music has survived into the present day, with his contributions to the Victorian musical theatre and to its sheet music industry".

His early music was mostly dance music, until he became musical director of the Strand Theatre. In 1865, in collaboration with FC Burnand, later to work with Arthur Sullivan, he produced Windsor Castle, a "historical opera burlesque" which, according to Scowcroft is probably the first English opera-bouffe, a form of comic opera, originally associated with Jacques Offenbach.

Burnand said of Musgrave, he had "no musical (or other) education and he could turn out a catchy popular tune, could score for a small orchestra, had a keen sense of humour and was a first-class stage manager". The latter comment suggests there might well have been three people trying to put their creative mark on St George. Musgrave became the lessee of the Theatre Royal Nottingham in 1873 and in 1878 began touring French operetta with his own company.

In terms of the cast, apart from Susie Vaughan, the sister of Kate, the main performers of note are WH Payne and his son Fred, though Lauri as Zazel, according to the Herald ad, "will perform with the stage traps and introduce some feats never before attempted at the Alexandra Palace".

The Weekly Herald advert gives perhaps just a sense of the pantomime. "The subject which Mr Emden has chosen for his Transformation Scene is 'Vertumna and the Swallows', in which some novel effects of a beautiful character will be developed. Mr Emden has carefully avoided what are known technically as carpenters' scenes, and has made each scene a 'set', thus producing a series of pictures such as are not usually seen in pantomimes.

"The Ballet Corps has been formed and superintended by Mr John Lauri, who is well-known in connection with his productions at the Alhambra Theatre. The chief ballet is entitled a 'Fete Champetre a la Watteau'. One of the most effective scenes will be 'The Village of laughing Waters', in which 'real water' will be effectively introduced.

"The great processional and spectacular scene will be Egyptian — the champions having been led to Egypt in search of adventure. In conclusion, to say that the comic scenes have been arranged and will be played by the Payne family, is to say that fun of the richest vein without a steak of coarseness will be assured."

It goes on to say the pantomime would open on 21 December and play daily at 3pm, and that "the Palace will be comfortably warmed".

Dick Whittington and his Cat

Christmas 1878
By G B O'Halloran
Nothing is known at the moment about this production or its writer, except that the script is in the library of New South Wales.

Harlequin Little Jack Horner or Goody Two Shoes and The Three Bears

Christmas 1879

Story	Frank Stainforth
New music	William Corri
Producer	TH Friend
Scenery	Thomas Rogers
Ballet	John Lauri
Comic scenes	WH Harvey (late of Drury Lane)
Demon Ignorance	Charles Coborn
Jack Horner	Caroline Parkes
Goody Two-Shoes	Miss George Edmonds
Fairy Commonsense	Miss Alice Clyfforde
Attendants	Misses Clara Hodgson, Kate Smith
Auricomus	Frank Stainforth
Principal danseuse(s)	Miss Luna (Lily Davis)
Mother Shipton	Mr Field
Little Boy Blue	Lilla Howard
Sir Graspall Gripper	WH Harvey
King Robin	CW Chamberlain
Harlequin	John Lauri
Columbine	Lily Davis
Pantaloon	Mr Beckenham

An advertisement for a public rehearsal in the Weekly Herald of 20 December 1879 gives a description of the scenes (though no details of scenes 8 and 10 are given). The story is a typical mash up of nursery rhyme and fairy tale elements. As the advert describes it: "The hero chosen for the Pantomime is 'Little Jack Horner', but with this has been interwoven the favourite old nursery legends of Little Goody Two-Shoes (who becomes the sweetheart of Jack), and the Three Bears."

Once again the opening scene uses the device of a group of people choosing the subject for a pantomime (to disguise the fantastic melting pot of the story elements, perhaps), but also introduces an interesting topical note with the appearance of Demon Ignorance as a strike agitator, who is of course "foiled in his dealings with the working men".

Scene 1: The Golden Halls of Auricomus

"We find tiny miners [children?] wielding pick and shovel in search of gold. To them enters the Demon Ignorance (Mr Charles Coborn), disguised as a strike agitator, and not unlike our old friend Ally Sloper, who urges them to put the screw on their tyrant master. The Fairy Commonsense (Miss Alice Clyfforde), with her attendants Amusement and Instruction (Miss Clara Hodgson and Miss Kate Smith) appears, and by magic power gives the miners a glimpse into futurity, to show the result of a strike.

"Auricomus, the monarch of the mine (Mr Frank Stainforth), is appealed to for help to furnish the Fairy Christmas Revels, and the subject of the Pantomime and its characters are determined upon."

Scene 2: The Peerless Palace of the Passing Hours

"After a brilliant procession of the Hours, Days, Weeks, Months and Seasons, Mr John Lauri's Seaweed Ballet takes place; Mdlle Luna being the principal danseuse, and Miss Lily Davis dancing a pas de deux with her."

Scene 3: Domino Castle, the home of Mother Shipton

"The action of the pantomime commences. Ignorance foiled in his dealings with the working men, has become a swell, and now applies to Mother Shipton to assist him in his designs upon Goody. They play a game with Goblin Dominoes to settle the question of whether or not the aid shall be given, and the Dame wins. The Queen of Hearts is here seen making her tarts, and the audacious robbery of the same by the Knave takes place, while a chorus to the air of 'The Harp that once' repeats the old nursery rhyme.

"Ignorance persuades Tommy Stout and Jemmy Green, two school boys who attend the school kept by Goody Two-Shoes, to attack Mother Shipton's dog. The Dame defends him, and is in turn protected from the mob by Jack. The old witch knows that Jack loves Goody, but that he cannot gain her hand because he is unable to read and write. To show her gratitude she promises to help him."

Scene 4: The cottage of Dame Crosspatch

"Dame Crosspatch, Jack's Aunt, who with her maids, illustrates 'Polly put the kettle on', 'Crosspatch drew the latch' and other well-known nursery rhymes. Her gossips arrive and Jack is discovered eating the historic Christmas pie. Mother Shipton teaches Jack his letters by calling forth a procession of representatives of the old familiar 'A was an Archer' series, in fact a most animated alphabet."

Scene 5: Outside the school-house of Goody Two-Shoes

"We see how this board-school teacher is worried by her pupils. Little Boy Blue (Miss Lilla Howard) asks for Goody's hand, but she has given her heart to Jack, and he is refused. Her severe landlord, Sir Graspall Gripper (Mr WH Harvey), calls for his rent, and offers also to marry the maiden. Jack saves her from the violence of the old man, but her goods are seized by his brokers.

"Ignorance teaches Goody to go and search in a certain Hawthorn Glade for hidden gold, in order that he may get her into his power. Mother Shipton to foil his wicked attempts, gives Jack the sword of sharpness, the shoes of swiftness, and the scarf of darkness, and sends him on his way after Goody to the Magic Wood."

Scene 6: Hawthorn Glade

"We are next shown Goody in the Hawthorn Glade. Ignorance ... is waiting to pounce upon the innocent Goody ... and Jack and Boy Blue who are close upon the heels of the damsel, are startled and terrified by the hideous sounds heard in the Haunted Forest."

Scene 7: Forest home of the Three Bears

"While they [The Three Bears] are out for a stroll, Goody drops in, tastes their porridge, sits in their chairs, and after trying the other, goes to sleep in the bed of the little bear. Here she is discovered and the monsters seizing her, determine to make her into a pie. She is scarcely beneath the crust when Jack rushes in, and, after a terrific struggle, conquers the bears.

"Ignorance causes the mists to descend, and so fogs Jack. The Fairy Amusement, however, places him in command of Mother Shipton's army from the Land of Toys, and sends him to King Robin de Bobbin's castle, where Goody has been conveyed by the demon."

Scene 9: The exterior of King Robin's castle

"The king (Mr CW Chamberlain) has a fair daughter, whom he wishes to get married and he locks her up till he finds a suiter in the cell with Goody. Boy Blue arrives, finds Goody, and falls in love with the princess.

"We are then shown the ramparts of the castle, Jack arrives with the army, and after a stirring speech, a paraphrase of the famous 'Once more unto the breach' and 'St Crispin's day' speeches in Henry V, the walls are stormed, King Robin's giants are killed, flames burst forth, the bastions are destroyed, and Jack is seen triumphant on the summit of the tower with Goody in his arms."

Scene 11: The home of Queen Mab

"The King and Ignorance, who have managed to get thoroughly drunk during the battle, console themselves with t'other bottle. The Demon becomes jovial, and says in song 'I can take a little drop now and then'. The Fairies reappear, and Ignorance becomes learned and chats in French; this is too much, and he is snuffed out. In Cloudland Jack sings his opinion upon things in general, and Mother Shipton joins the lovers' hands.

"We are then transported to the home of Queen Mab, the gorgeous transformation scene, which introduces cataracts of prismatic waters, with nymphs reclining beneath the moonlight fernery, in the Jewelled Home of the Fairy Queen." (A watery ending again.)

None of the creative team appears to be of great note. Frank Stainforth seems to be another Victorian jobbing writer and actor, who is only remembered today as co-author with James Willing of the play The Ruling Passion. He was also credited with the story for Alexandra Palace's Puss in Boots. William Corri may be a descendent of the famous musical Corri family and was also to provide music for Triumph of Summer and Puss in Boots.

The best known name today is Charles Coborn, then in his mid-twenties, who would later make a music hall career out of two songs: Two Lovely Black Eyes, which he adapted from an existing song in 1886; and Fred Gilbert's 1892 song, The Man Who Broke the Bank at Monte Carlo. Coborn, who died in 1945 aged 91, estimated he sang Man Who Broke the Bank some 250,000 times during his career — and could do so in 14 languages.

In an age before mechanical reproduction — records, radio or TV and film — artists could tour with their material and use it over and over again. Later in his life Coborn recorded the song and appeared in films.

A separate report in the Seven Sisters and Finsbury Park Journal says that Jack Horner was played by Miss Caroline Parkes and Goody Two-Shoes by Miss George Edmonds.

"Despite financial difficulties, it was a spectacular production," according to Carrington. He quotes the North Middlesex Chronicle: "The grand transformation scene by Mr Thomas Rogers entitled the Home of Queen Mab is a splendid piece of fairy-like workmanship, embracing the most wonderful combination of real water, ferns, fairies and flowers; and such was the splendour that some of the rougher element in the top gallery could not restrain their emotion at the sight of so much beautiful effect and artistic resplendence, but gave vent to it in whistling and hurrahing."

That presumably would have taken their minds off any thoughts of going on strike. Perhaps an added reason the top balcony was later removed was to deter the "rougher element". The class undertones chime with the reference to Charles Coborn's agitator being like Ally Sloper — an early cartoon character introduced in the 1860s in Judy magazine, a rival of Punch, who was a red-nosed idle chancer often caught sloping down alleys to avoid his creditors.

The Weekly Herald gave its verdict on the pantomime a week after it advertised it: "We last week gave an outline of the Grand Christmas Pantomime announced for performance at the Alexandra Palace. It was produced last Saturday at a public rehearsal, in the presence of a large audience, and all who witnessed it pronounced it to be one of the best — if not the best — ever produced at the Palace.

"It is full of life and fun, while the familiar nursery legends with which it abounds render it especially interesting to juveniles. We are introduced not only to Little Jack Horner (who is the hero of the piece), but Goody-two-Shoes and the Three Bears are also to the fore; while the alphabet in verse — 'A was an Archer' — and so forth; the Mouse that ran up the clock; Little Boy Blue; Dame Cross-patch; King Robin de Bobbin; and we know not how many other heroes of nursery lore are introduced to the audience.

"A very pretty ballet is introduced, in a splendid scene depicting the Peerless Palace of the Passing Hours, in which Madlle Luna, Madlle Stella , and Miss Lily Davis take part. The Lilliputian Army of horse and foot fairly fill the stage; and their attack upon the castle of the greedy Robin de Bobbin, 'who ate a cow, who ate a calf, who ate a butcher and a half', which ends in the castle being blown up and demolished, is calculated to fill the youthful mind with delight and wonder.

"The transformation scene is of a gorgeous description; it is entitled 'The Home of Queen Mab' and introduces a cataract of real water, with fairies reclining on its banks, while behind rises a temple of nacre which opens and discloses other fairies, and on all sides other fairies gradually rise until the stage is like that ante-chamber in Buddah's Palace described in the 'Light of Asia'.

"The comic business [the Harlequinade] of course follows, and it is of a character calculated to send our juvenile friends into ecstasies. Altogether, the Pantomime deserves to be the popular 'hit' of the season."

But it was not enough to save Bertram and Roberts, the lessees of the Palace, Carrington adds: "The pantomime was Bertram and Roberts last attempt to bring prosperity to the Palace. At the end of January 1880, it was announced that the Palace and park was to be let on lease from 5 May."

The Triumph of Summer or the Golden Months of the Year

July 1880
(Masque)

Producer/Director	TH Friend
Music	WH Montgomery and W Corri
Scenery	Mr Schonberg
Properties	Mr Lightfoot
Machinery	Mr Blanchard
Dresses	Mr and Mrs Stinchcombe
Ballet	John Lauri
King Winter	Aynsley Cooke
Sunbeam	Nellie Power (Perm of F Villiers esq)
Spring	Nelly Moon
Queen of the May	Grace Beverley
Robin Hood	Caroline Parkes
Schoolboy	John Lauri
Charity Boy	The Great Little Rowella
Will Scarlett	J Beckenham
Jack Pudding	Dolph Rowella
Danseuses	Mdlles Luna, Stella; Sisters Elliott

No review of of the production has yet been found, but the production team led by TH Friend was a regular one of this period, apart from the unknown Mr Schonberg responsible for the scenery and the addition of dance-tune composer WH Montgomery to the music credits.

Aynsley Cooke is, almost certainly, the brother of Furneaux Cook, a noted Savoyard — one of the regular singers of Gilbert and Sullivan operas at the Savoy Theatre.

The most notable member of the cast is Nelly Power (sometimes written Nellie), who was to become a music hall star with an act that mimicked George Leybourne — Champagne Charlie- caricaturing dandies. Her most famous song, written for her by George Ware, was The Boy I love Is up in the Gallery. (Hopefully, not with the lower kind.)

Puss in Boots or The Butterflies' Ball and The Grasshoppers' Feast

Christmas 1880

Story	Frank Stainforth
New music	William Corri
Scenery	Messrs William Brew, Lancaster, Johnson
Producer/Director	TH Friend
Orchestra	JT Haines
Ballet	John Lauri
Comic scenes	Decona
Dresses	Mr & Mrs Stinchcombe
Properties	Mr Lightfoot
Machinery	Mr Blanshard
Gas Arrangements	Mr Blackwell
Dame Trot	Mr M Bentley
Mother Hubbard	Mr J Cole
Dame Wiggins	Mr W Morgan
The Cheerful Cheshire Cat	Master Eugene Devani
Mother Hubbard's Dog	Mr Aynsley Cooke, Junior
Dame Wiggins' Goose	Mr Aynsley Cooke, Junior
Demon Indigestion	Frank Stainforth
King Nonsense	Miss Lilian English
Burlesque (henchman)	Miss Marie Temple
Pantomime (henchman)	Miss Daisy Herve

The Griffin	Charles Raynor
Fairy Queen Papilionette	Miss Grace Howard
Silverwing	Miss Florence Herve
Danseuse	Mdlle Forna (libretto gives first name as Irma) von Rokoy
Richard "The Sulky"	Edwin Granger
Robin "The Silly"	Mr Anthony
Lawyer Shark	Mr Decona
Jocelyn	Miss Clara St Leger
Puss in Boots	Miss Caroline Parkes
Jack O'Lantern	Mr George Lauri
King Kockahoop	Mr JF Brian
Queen	Mrs JF Brian
Prince Perfect	Miss Marie Temple
Prince Precious	Miss Elma Bronte
Prince Delicious	Miss Clara Bronte
Prince Pet	Miss Hurley
Flunkeybus (Chamberlain)	Mr J Anthony
Princess Prettypet	Miss Lettie (libretto spells first name as Letty) Lind
Clown	Mr Decona
Harlequin	George Lauri
Columbine/Harlequina	Miss Kitchen / Miss Clement
Pantaloon	Mr Beckenham (libretto gives name as Mr J Beckingham)
Policeman	Mr Sugar

The libretto of the production at Alexandra Palace lists 13 scenes:

Scene 1	The cottage of Dame Trott at the foot of the Katskill Mountains
Scene 2	The moonlit haunt in the mushroom glade, by the side of the silver sea
Scene 3	Muddlehead's Mill
Scene 4	The road to Blunderland
Scene 5	Blunderland
Scene 6	The palace of King Kockahoop
Scene 7	The cornfields near the domains of King Kockahoop
Scene 8	The courtyard of the castle of Grimguffin
Scene 9	Dining hall of the ogre's castle

Scene 10	The courtyard
Scene 11	The Grand Transformation Scene, The birth of Venus
Scene 12	Tailor's and milliner's and doctor's shops
Scene 13	The country barber's

Despite a successful summer — over 1.1 million visitors to the Palace in six months — the lessee Mr Willing was reported to have made a loss and did not extend his lease after September, so yet another management was in charge for the 1880 pantomime.

We have one report of Puss in Boots, in the Weekly Herald of 31 December 1880, from which to gauge the production.

"When the curtain rises we find Dame Trot (Mr M Bentley) with her feline followers around her, in her cottage at the foot of the Katskill Mountains. Here she welcomes Mother Hubbard and her famous dogs, with Dame Wiggins and her equally famous goose. The three old ladies are about to determine upon the subject for the Christmas entertainment when they are interrupted by the Demon Indigestion (Mr Frank Stainforth) who threatens to bring the festivities to a dismal end.

"He in turn is confronted by King Nonsense (Miss Lilian English), who, with his attendants Burlesque and Pantomime, comes to aid the concoctors of the play. The subject is chosen, and Indigestion, in revenge, brings the Griffin (Mr Charles Raynor) from the front of the Law Courts, and makes him the Ogre in their Pantomime.

"The second scene brings us to the Moonlit Haunt in the Mushroom Glade, by the side of the Silver Sea. Here the fairy queen, Papilionette (Miss Grace Howard) tells Dame Trot and King Nonsense to seek their hero at Muddlehead's Mill, and invites the characters to the Butterflies' Ball and the Grasshoppers' Feast.

"Here we have the Brilliant Ballet of Bright Butterflies, especially arranged by Mr John Lauri, in which Mdlle Forna von Rokoy dances the famous Pas de Papillons.

"We are then conducted to Muddlehead's Mill, [Scene 3] where we find that old Muddlehead's will is to be read. The eldest nephew Richard (Mr Grainger) has the mill and farm, the second Robin (Mr Anthony), the donkey, while to the third Jocelyn (Miss Clara St. Leger), nothing is left but the cat.

"Jocelyn, however, has been generous to Old Dame Trot, and she teaches him his letters, and changes his cat into the tiger, Puss in Boots

(Miss Caroline Parkes), who promises to lead him to fortune.

"On the road to Blunderland [Scene 4], Indigestion is foiled by Mother Wiggins' Goose (Mr Aynesley Cooke, jnr), and in Blunderland itself [Scene 5], a place to which the juvenile offenders of Fairy Land are transported by Sir Vernon Harcourt of that realm, Jocelyn engages the light-headed and light-heeled Jack-o'-Lantern (Mr George Lauri), as his valet.

"In the next scene [Scene 6] we are taken to the court of King Kockahoop (Mr JF Brian), who with his Queen (Mrs JF Brian), are endeavouring to marry their rich niece, Princess Prettypet (Miss Lettie Lind), to their son Prince Perfect (Miss Marie Temple).

[Scene 7] "The king and court go hunting, and Jack-o'-Lantern comes to grief in the ditch.

"The Ground Game Bill has destroyed all the king's game, and Puss opportunely arrives with a present of hares and rabbits. Puss tells the king that his master, who is bathing in the river, is drowning and that his clothes are stolen. The king comes to the rescue and Jocelyn enters as the Marquis de Carabas.

"Jocelyn and the Princess fall in love at first sight, and while the court is feasting, and the rustics dancing, the Ogre arrives and after a vain struggle to capture the Princess, carries off Jack-o'-Lantern.

[Scene 8] "The Ogre returns to his castle, where Jack is promoted to the office of cook. Puss arrives and contrives to enter the castle.

[Scene 9] "The Ogre has his dinner, catches cold, and after some chemical experiments in which Jack nearly blows up the place, is induced by Puss to give an exhibition of his skill. He transports himself into an enormous giant, then into one of the Midgets from the Egyptian Hall, next he appears as the British Lion, but on becoming a mouse he is seized and killed by puss.

"The king and court arrive and are welcomed by Jocelyn, and his majesty is about to bestow his niece's hand upon the young man when Indigestion once more interrupts the general harmony.

"In the next scene [Scene 10] the characters rehearse the entertainments about to be given in honour of the wedding, and Jocelyn destroys the power of Indigestion by confessing the secret of his birth. Puss is about to be hanged when Papilionette arrives, saves him, and conducts the characters to Fairyland, where they witness Mr Brew's Grand Transformation Scene, entitled 'The Birth of Venus' [Scene 11]."

Scene 11 includes "The Harlequinade arranged by The Great Decona", according to the libretto.

The libretto describes Scene 12, Tailor's and milliner's and doctor's shops:

"Clown outside Sloshy and Swill's doctors shop — Medicine penny a pailful, pills for nothing — Clown goes in for a tightener, and meets with Mother Rumptytump coming out, and knocks down Jimmy Chummey — upsets the wooden-legged sailor, row and fight takes place with the butcher and the baker; the butcher hits the baker one in the bread-basket, that knocks him into the chest of eggs twenty-four for a shilling"

It also describes Scene 13, The country barber's:

"Hallo! hi, what a lark! — Sausages fried in ice all the year round — Clown takes Barber's Shop — Three shaves a penny, find your own soap and razor — Dreadful row between the Policeman and Clown — Policeman gets blown up — Subscriptions sent for his wife and family."

Guests at the Butterflies' Ball and Grasshoppers' Feast (Scene 2) are described in the libretto:

"Messieurs and Mesdames Mole, Beetle, Lizard, Snail, Bee, Dragonfly, Spider, Dormouse, Hornet, Wasp, Frog etc. N.B. No flies were invited, because they will swarm on to the dishes before other people are helped, which is not good manners."

The Weekly Herald reports that George Lauri was a "nimble and graceful Harlequin" and that the band "has been greatly augmented", with the whole production managed by Mr TH Friend "who has invented and arranged the stage business of the piece".

Once again, despite the management change, the production team has a familiar look to it, with Messrs William Brew and Johnson returning to scenery duty, with another story and acting role from Frank Stainforth. The most notable cast member is Letty Lind, who would in later decades become one of the profession's highest paid performers.

Caroline Parkes, the principal boy, was the sister of a famous actress of the late Victorian and Edwardian eras, Henrietta Hobson, and wife of a famous Harlequin, Charles Fenton. She is often credited as working on the same productions as TH Friend, at various theatres.

Hop O' My Thumb or Harlequin No-Body, Some-Body, Busy-Body, and the Wicked Ogre with the Seven-League Boots

Christmas 1881

Producer/Director	George Conquest Jnr
Story	Frank W Green
Scenery	Messrs Grieve & Son; Messrs Thomas Rogers & Son
Composer/arranger	Meyer Lutz
Ballet	Madame Katti Lanner
Dresses	Mr and Mrs Stinchcombe
Properties	Mr Lightfoot
Machinery	Mr Blanchard
Gas arrangements	Mr Steadman
Limelights	Mr C Martin
Assistant stage manager	Mr Reuben Inch

King Nobody/Ogreiferous	George Conquest jnr
Prince Fizz	Miss Patti Mortimer
Prince Chic	Miss Annie Robe
Dame Noodle	Sam Wilkinson
Servants	R Inch, H Lemaire
King Colchicum	Matt Gordon
Princess Prettyeyes	Miss Lilian Adair
Lollipop (tiger)	Miss M Brabazon
Hop O' My Thumb	Miss Katie Barry
Gaffer Noodle	Watty Brunton
Fairy Busybody	Miss Minne Inch
Fairy Somebody	Miss Constance Brabazon
Harlequinade:	
Clown	Reuben Inch
Harlequin	Mr C Bartram
Pantaloon	H Lemaire
Columbine	Miss Le Brun

Nymphs, Fairies, Courtiers, Pages, Peasants, Guards, Demons, etc, "in reckless profusion"

Scene 1:	Nobody's Land
Scene 2:	The Village of Bizzibeedom in the Year A1. Rustic Revels, introducing a Novel Ballet of Gleaners

Scene 3:   The Long Skirts of the Woodland
Scene 4:   The Fairy Forest of Ferns. Grand Fairy Ballet
Scene 5:   Diorama on the Road to Ogre Land
Scene 6:   The Ogre's Bed Chamber
Scene 7:   Pretty Landscape in Pantomimia
Scene 8:   Palace of King Colchicum
Scene 9:   Frost-bound Glade. The duel in the snow
Scene 10:   The Grand Transformation: The Abode of Flora, the Goddess of Flowers; Harlequinade
Scene 11:   The Poultry, 1881 Prince's Restaurant (Jones & Barber's) Chemist's Shop (Perry Davis's Painkiller), and Wolff's (the Tailor's)
Scene 12:   Butcher's, Tailors, and Cheesemongers
Scene 13:   Shadow Pantomime
                Finale

The credits (from the Weekly Herald of 30 December 1881 and the AP daily programme) have echoes of the first Alexandra Palace pantomime in what would be the last of the era. Producer and director George Conquest Jnr follows in his father's footsteps and returns as both actor and in overall charge of proceedings. Messrs Grieve and Son, the original stage and set designers are also back, sharing the scene credits with Thomas Rogers & Son, who were responsible for Little Jack Horner.

These were augmented by a distinguished composer and choreographer in Meyer Lutz and Katti Lanner.

Lutz was born in Bavaria the son of a music professor and came to Britain in 1848 at the age of 19. His older brother, Baron John Lutz, would later become prime minister under King Ludwig II of Bavaria (the Mad King). Meyer Lutz, as others, began as a church organist before becoming a theatrical conductor, at the Surrey and Royalty theatres, later becoming musical director of the Gaiety Theatre. He conducted Thespis, the first Gilbert & Sullivan comic opera, in 1871.

Meanwhile, he composed one-act and grand operas, cantatas and incidental music, as well as conducting concerts and holding piano recitals. He was, as were many composers of the day, prolific in many fields, from opera to burlesque. He has links with other Alexandra Palace performers through his marriage to first Elizabeth Cook, then her sister Emily, the sisters of the bass Thomas Aynsley Cook.

Katti Lanner was born in Vienna and was the daughter of the court director of ballet. She toured Europe with the Vienna Ballet Company and first played at Drury Lane in 1871. She returnd to England in 1875 to take over the National Training School of Dancing, producing ballets and pantomimes, and training dancers. Dancers from the school appear in Hop O' My Thumb. She is credited with reviving the art of ballet in Britain.

But even her distinguished input was not enough to save Alexandra Palace. This was to be the last Victorian pantomime. In 1882 the financial problems which had beset Alexandra Palace from the start would overwhelm it. It would continue to open intermittently over the next two decades but its original ambitions for the Theatre — to which the pantomimes seem central — would no longer be pursued.

The Operas

Examination of the operas performed at the Alexandra Palace Theatre seems to support the conjecture that the Theatre was designed mainly for musical theatre, its elongated shape, whether by design or accident, better suited to music and spectacle than spoken drama.

Between 1875 and 1888, and the long-term closure of the Palace, a wide range of operas were performed, ranging from opera-bouffe or comic opera, through European operetta and Gilbert and Sullivan, to the canon of dramatic opera, from Mozart to Donizetti. It would provide a staple if not the mainstay of performance in the Theatre — indeed in 1879 it seems that virtually the only performances were of opera.

The first Alexandra Palace Programmes of Arrangements for both first and second Palaces state the purpose of the theatre was for "operatic and dramatic performances" (in that order). Mostly the operas seem to have been performed in English and reports of performances throughout this period refer to their success.

The Weekly Herald commented in October 1875, after the first season of autumn operas: "Of the many varied attractions which have been provided at Alexandra Palace, none have been more uniformly successful than the series of operas in English."

The same paper commented of a performance of the popular opera Maritana the following year: "The opera met a highly favourable reception, and the principal artists received the usual tribute in the shape of divers 'calls' before the curtain."

And the Southwark Standard reported of the performance of another popular opera, The Bohemian Girl, in autumn 1888, not long before the Palace's long closure: "The performance was a decided success. The old and favourite songs being vociferously encored."

Our current research has been able to identify about 60 different productions, of some three-dozen operas by 22 different composers. At least half a dozen production companies were involved, with two productions under the supervision of their composers.

The most performed composers were Michael William Balfe, with five operas (The Bohemian Girl, Rose of Castille, Satanella, The Puritan's Daughter, The Sleeping Queen), followed by Jacques Offenbach (Breaking the Spell, The Brigands, Genevieve de Brabant, Orpheus in the Underworld), Daniel Auber (Fra Diavolo, The Crown Diamonds), Gaetano Donizetti (Lucia di Lammermoor, Elixir of Love), Giuseppe Verdi (Il Trovatore, Il Traviata), Gilbert and Sullivan (HMS Pinafore, Trial by Jury), Rossini (Cinderella, Barber of Seville), and Mozart (Don Giovanni, Marriage of Figaro).

Those represented by one opera were: Louis Diehl (The Elfin Tree), HB Farnie (Nemesis), Charles Lecocq (La Fille de Madame Angot), Charles Gounod (Faust), Vincenzo Bellini (La Sonnambula), William Vincent Wallace (Maritana), Jules Benedict (Lily of Killarney), Carl Maria von Weber (Der Freischutz), George Macfarren (Robin Hood), Giacomo Mayerbeer (Dinorah), Charles Dibden (The Waterman), Bizet (Carmen), Edward Solomon (Billee Taylor) and Beethoven (Fidelio).

Jules Benedict and Edward Solomon both conducted — and possibly directed — the performances of their respective operas. It is unlikely that this list is exhaustive, but it nevertheless gives a good overview of the kind of work performed in the Theatre.

According to our current research, the most popular operas, with six different productions each, were Maritana and The Bohemian Girl. These are followed by Faust (five), La Sonnambula (five), Il Trovatore (four), Lily of Killarney (two) and Don Giovanni (two).

Many, if not most, of the operas seem to have been produced by the Carl Rosa Opera Company, but other companies are identified, including the Strand (Theatre) Company and Blanche Cole Company, while Valentine Smith, a principal at the Drury Lane Theatre, is credited as producer for the later operas. In addition, Emily Soldene is credited with appearing as Carmen in her own production of Bizet's opera. The presence of Cole and Soldene in the creative credits suggests a more powerful position for women in opera, where divas tended to be the main crowd pullers.

The first production for which we have a report is Offenbach's one-act operetta, Breaking the Spell, performed on the opening night of the (second) Theatre, Monday 3 May 1875, when it was on a programme with the spectacle, Minerva. If it was performed in English — the report of the concert in The Era is unclear, but it names a duet in English — then it may have been to a libretto by HB (Henry Brougham) Farnie, whose own opera Nemesis was produced at the Theatre later.

The Era reported: "The three characters of the operetta were sustained as follows: Jenny Wood, Miss Gertrude Ashton, who won considerable fame by her operatic performances at the Alexandra Theatre, Camden Town; Peter Bloom, the lover, Mr Wilford Morgan, one of the most competent English tenors; and the old Chelsea pensioner Matthew, Mr Richard Temple."

"It was well adapted for the occasion and went uncommonly well," it judged. It also commended the conductor, Mr Weist Hill. "A more competent or experienced artiste it would have been difficult to find."

The next opera performance we have a record of is The Elfin Tree, by Louis Diehl, performed on Whit Monday 1875, two and a half weeks after the second Palace opened. It was the opening performance in the Theatre's programme for that day, which included two performances of the spectacle Minerva and a performance of the farce, The Area Belle.

However, the AP Programme of Arrangements for 1875-76 reported that during May (the Palace reopened on 1 May 1875), "Opera Comique and Ballet Divertissement" would take place in the theatre daily, except Saturdays. So Breaking The Spell and The Elfin Tree may have been performed on several occasions.

Little is known about The Elfin Tree or Louis Diehl. Diehl was a French violinist and songwriter whose wife has a claim to fame as the most famous musical daughter of the Essex town of Thurrock. Alice M Diehl was a concert pianist who later wrote at least 38 unheralded novels, but her autobiography, The True Story of My Life, and another memoir, Musical Memories, are important sources of information on performers in the late 19th century.

Notable in the cast, were Aynsley Cook and Henry Nordblom, who both made regular appearances at Alexandra Palace. Indeed, the whole musical Cook family seem to have taken to the Alexandra Palace stage at some point, with Aynsley and Aynsley Jnr both appearing in pantomime at the theatre. It's not clear who the production company was.

The next production for which we have details was HB Farnie's Nemesis, a similar operetta performed by the Strand Company in August of that year. The company may have produced The Elfin Tree — although the opera was also in the repertoire of Carl Rosa. Or perhaps these opening productions were mounted by the Alexandra Palace itself.

The Strand Theatre, demolished in 1905 to make way for Aldwych tube station, was successful in the 1860s and 70s with burlesque, popular operettas and pantomime — Widow Twankey made her first appearance there. HB Farnie was a typical jobbing actor, musician and writer. A later review describes Nemesis as "an operatic extravaganza". It adds: "The music has been culled from various composers, among whom may be mentioned Offenbach, Lecocq, Planquette, Von Suppe, Meyer Lutz and Florian Pascal; and the result, if patchy, is on the whole very pleasing."

The Weekly Herald commented of the production at the Palace: "The performance gave great satisfaction, some of the songs being encored."

Songs were encored too in the production of Lecocq's comic opera, La Fille de Madame Angot, which followed Nemesis the same month, when the theatre "was crowded in every part".

September 1875 saw the first full season of opera, as promised in the AP programme for 1875-76. The first Programme Of Arrangements, published at the opening of the second Palace that May, explained: "Feeling the importance of producing operas in English in the most complete and efficient manner, the directors have entered into an arrangement with Mr Carl Rosa, who has been for some time engaged in England and in Italy in forming an operatic company of the highest class."

It went on: "These operas will be given in the theatre in the months of September and October. The company will be precisely the same as that which will appear during those months at the Princess's Theatre, and the operas will be supported by numerous chorus and ballet. The repertoire will include two operas new to England."

The Carl Rosa Opera Company has an important place in opera history in Britain, particularly of opera sung in English. According to the Guardian on his death in 1889, Carl Rosa "lifted opera out of the slough of despond in which it was found in 1875" and showed that English opera could be an artistic and financial success.

According to the musicologist Sir George Grove in 1880: "The careful way in which the pieces are put on the stage, the number of rehearsals, the eminence of the performers and the excellence of the performers have begun to bear their legitimate fruit, and the Carl Rosa Opera Company bids fair to become a permanent institution."

The company continued through wars and financial problems for the next 90 years, before the final curtain descended at the Prince's Theatre in 1960. However, the company was revived in 1997 with a base in the north-east of England and continues to tour.

Carl August Nicolas Rosa (Rose in the original German — he changed the spelling because the British mispronounced it as the flower), was born in Hamburg and was a child prodigy on the violin, touring Scotland with great success for four years in his early teens. He was trained in Leipzig — where he made a lasting friendship with

Arthur Sullivan — and Paris, and first formed a touring company with his wife, the Scottish soprano Euphrosyne Parepa, in New York in 1869.

In 1872 they returned to Britain, and Carl Rosa Opera made its debut with Maritana in Manchester in 1873, then touring the country. His wife died in childbirth in 1874, but Carl continued, and the company's first London season opened at the Princess's Theatre in September 1875 — so the first Alexandra Palace season was also part of that London debut. The first production was Mozart's Marriage of Figaro, but there is no current record of that being played at the Alexandra Palace Theatre.

The first Carl Rosa opera we have a report of at the Palace is Gounod's Faust, in the company's first autumn season, in September, which attracted "an enormous audience that filled the theatre". Ostava Torriani as Marguerite "produced rounds of applause which necessitated her reappearance after the fall of the curtain upon the second act". Faust was played by Fred Packard and Mephistopheles by Aynsley Cook — Mrs Aynsley Cook played Martha. Also among the cast who would make many appearances at the Palace were Lucy Franklein, Mr Ludwig (another performer lost to Victorian formality) and Arthur Howell.

Faust was followed by one of the most popular operas of the time: Balfe's The Bohemian Girl. The opera was to be produced at least half a dozen times at Alexandra Palace. Balfe, along with Wallace, composer of Maritana, were two of the very few composers of music in England to receive any recognition outside Britain in the 19th century. A statement carefully phrased, because both were Irish.

Balfe was born in Dublin, moving to Wexford as a child where he played violin for his father's dancing classes. In 1823, at just 15, he moved to London and joined the orchestra of the Theatre Royal, Drury Lane. In 1825 he moved to Rome and started composing, becoming, it is said, a protégé of Rossini. In 1827 he appeared as Figaro in The Barber of Seville in Paris. His first success as a composer in London was The Siege of Rochelle at Drury Lane in 1835.

The Bohemian Girl was premiered at Drury Lane in November 1843 and it ran for over 100 nights. Productions followed in New York, Dublin, Sydney and Vienna and around the world. As well as German and French versions, there was an Italian version La Zingara, which was often produced around the world, including in Anglophone countries.

The plot is taken from a story by Cervantes, La Gitanilla. The Bohemian Girl revolves around the love of a Polish noble Thaddeus for Arline, daughter of the Count of Arnheim . Their plans are thwarted by a Gypsy Queen, who is killed in the last reel and the world is put to rights. It's hard not to see great similarities with the pantomime plots of the age, if a little less fantastical.

A silent film version with Ellen Terry and Ivor Novello was shot in 1922 and a full-length comedy version with Laurel and Hardy was made in 1936. The opera stayed in the standard repertoire until the 1930s, but is only occasionally performed today. Its best known song, I Dreamt I Dwelt in Marble Halls, has been widely recorded, including by Dame Joan Sutherland and the modern Irish singer Enya. But Balfe is best remembered today, if at all, for the much parodied song, Come into the Garden, Maud.

According to Carrington, Wallace's Maritana was also played in this first season at Alexandra Palace — along with Friedrich von Flotow's Martha — but our current research has found no further details of these. Wallace's opera was certainly performed the following year, and alongside The Bohemian Girl was the most popular at the Palace.

The composer of Maritana was born William Wallace, the son of a regimental bandmaster, in Waterford, and became an accomplished pianist and violinist. He was presumably a Protestant, because the father of the girl he was to marry in 1831 — a pupil at the Ursuline convent in Dublin where Wallace was a piano teacher — consented to the marriage on the condition that Wallace became a Catholic and added Vincent to his name.

After many years travelling to Australia, New Zealand, and Latin America — he later claimed to have gone tiger-hunting in India and whaling in the South Seas — William Vincent Wallace toured the United States, where he helped to found the New York Philharmonic Society. He returned to London in 1845, giving many piano recitals. Maritana, the first of his six operas, was first performed the same year at Drury Lane, conducted by Jules Benedict. Productions followed in Vienna and at Covent Garden.

Maritana is taken from a contemporary French play based on the character of Don Cesar de Bazan in Victor Hugo's Ruy Blas. In the opera, unlucky Don Cesar is sentenced to death for duelling by the King of Spain. Don Jose, a thoroughly bad lot, offers Cesar a "soldier's death" if he will marry a veiled woman — intending to make Maritana a nobleman's widow. But at the wedding feast, Lazarillo, a boy helped by Don Cesar, removes all the bullets from the execution squad's guns and Don Cesar merely feigns death and escapes.

Eventually he falls in love with Maritana, kills Don Jose and becomes governor of Valencia. The prison love story is cited as the inspiration for the similar plot in Gilbert and Sullivan's Yeomen Of The Guard. It was the first opera produced by the Carl Rosa Opera Company and remained popular until the 1930s. It also gets a mention from James Joyce in both Ulysses and Dubliners.

Next in the series of Palace operas was Auber's Fra Diavolo, with Henry Nordblom in the title role ("his songs were enthusiastically received"), and a cast including Julia Gaylord — who also appeared in The Elfin Tree, suggesting that earlier productions may have been produced by Carl Rosa also — Aynsley Cook, Mr Ludwig and Arthur Howell. "The piece was capitally put on the boards, the scenery and effects being first rate," according to the Weekly Herald.

This was followed by Bellini's La Sonnambula, feauturing the soprano Rose Hersee. Hersee was the daughter of Henry Hersee, a critic for the Observer, and a librettist and translator of Carmen and Aida. She toured America with the Parepa-Rosa Opera Company and became a founding member of the Carl Rosa Company back in Britain. She also later formed her own opera company. The Times on her death in 1924 said that her performance as Susanna in the Marriage of Figaro was the best ever heard in the English language.

Offenbach's opera-bouffe, The Brigands, completed the first season.

Rose Hersee returned to the Palace in July 1876 to play Arline in The Bohemian Girl. Thaddeus was played by George Perren, with two other cast members who were to become Palace regulars, George Fox and George Harvey. It's not clear if this was a Carl Rosa production.

The autumn 1876 Carl Rosa season brought back a production of the ever-popular Maritana, with Cora Stuart in the lead role, and company regulars such as Nordblom, Ludwig, Cook and Howell.

The Herald was on this occasion more critical. While paying Stuart a slightly backhanded compliment for her Maritana — she "promises with further study to become an ornament to her profession" — it went on: "Miss Stuart sings cantabile phrases with perfect smoothness and steadiness of delivery; but when she attempts to produce effects which do not lie within her means the result is an appreciable loss of power." And in the extended length of the theatre auditorium, that was a distinct drawback.

But the Herald was more generally grumpy, complaining: "The chorus did their work ably, but the band was much too loud, notoriously in the brass, the continued din of which was deafening." Ouch. But the audience didn't seem to agree, offering "the usual tribute of divers 'calls' before the curtain".

Cora Stuart, then just 19, seems to have decided against too much further study and widened her field of work. After 1890 she became best known for appearances in a one-act musical comedy sketch, The Fair Equestrienne, which for many years she toured around the music halls. In a magazine interview in 1894 she described her career from grand opera to music hall. "I have done the whole round — made my first appearance in grand opera; played nearly all the comedies written by my father-in-law, the late TW Robertson; made hits in Pinero comedy; been in melodrama, farce, farcical comedy; and now you behold me 'on at the halls."

In case anyone should see that as a fall from grace she added: "I must say I prefer the variety stage to any other. One thing, the audiences are so awfully good." She died in 1940.

The rest of the 1876 Carl Rosa season seems to be mainly a repeat of the previous year's programme, with performances of Faust, Fra Diavolo and The Bohemian Girl. According to a report in the Weekly Herald, operatic performances by the company were given twice a week. Whether the planned two-month season lasted until the end of October is unclear. On 16 October a petition for bankruptcy was presented by the Alexandra Palace Company, following which the Palace closed until the next May.

The Palace reopened on 10 May 1877 with new lessees (Bertram and Roberts) and a new manager (WH Jones). A programme of daily events at the Palace refers to a series of operas, under Mr George Perren, and the Weekly Herald reported in June that "Operas and plays are almost daily performed in the theatre".

But the only opera we currently have a report for in 1877 is Verdi's Il Trovatore, at the end of May. Some of the cast had appeared in the production of The Bohemian Girl in the summer of 1876, including George Perren (Manrico in Trovatore), George Fox (Count di Luna), George Harvey (Ruiz) and Miss Palmer (Azucena).

Perhaps the most significant cast member was Richard Temple (Ferrando), who later the same year created the part of Sir Marmaduke Pointdextre in the first production of Gilbert and Sullivan's The Sorcerer, produced by Richard D'Oyly Carte. Thereafter he became a G&S regular, creating and performing most of the bass-baritone parts in their operas over the next couple of decades.

Temple was to return to Alexandra Palace the following year. In June 1878, he appeared as Don Pedro in Balfe's Rose of Castille. He is billed as appearing "by permission of Mr D'Oyly Carte", and he was also credited as producer and director of the opera. The cast also included Rose Hersee, Lucy Franklein, and the Georges, Fox and Harvey.

The conductor was also a musician and composer of some later distinction. Frederic Archer moved to the United States in 1880, where among his achievements was the establishment of one of the world's great orchestras, the Pittsburgh Symphony Orchestra.

The AP programmes advertise three operas in the autumn season, Maritana, with the title role sung by Rose Hersee; La Sonnambula, with Blanche Cole as Amina; and another production of Maritana, in November, with Arabella Smythe in the lead role (again conducted by Frederic Archer). Also credited as one of the cast (as the Marquis) is a Mr Friend — who may be the same as the stage manager for all three productions, Mr TH Friend.

Friend appears to be one of the key people at the Alexandra Palace Theatre in this period, being credited as stage manager or stage director for many of the productions over the next three years, including pantomimes. He seems to have begun his career as a stage manager in the 1860s, first at Astley's Theatre and at the Lyceum.

A short biography appears on the Scottish Opera website, as a result of his having been acting manager, designer and director on a number of productions for the Edinburgh Opera, a forerunner of Scottish Opera. "TH Friend was a well-known manager both in opera and straight theatre. For many years he played a key role in the Carl Rosa Company. He and Mr H Bruce became owners when Augustus Harris (who had been heavily involved following Carl Rosa's death) focused his efforts on Covent Garden."

Then it concludes with the understatement: "We have still to form a full picture of his career." Such a picture would tell us a lot about the Alexandra Palace Theatre too, particularly, perhaps, about the mounting of the productions, the use of the machinery, and the production companies and stage hands who worked the stage. At the moment we have little information on backstage operations.

A little coda to the AP programme reveals the Palace's long-standing concern about fire risk. "A smoking café will be found in the North-east Tower. A bell will be rung in the café two minutes before the commencement of each act of the opera. In order to avoid all risk of fire-accident, visitors are requested to aid the executive in limiting the right to smoke to the Tower base."

Productions in the theatre in 1879 were almost entirely operas. First off in March the Palace was treated to a performance of Lily of

Killarney, produced by its composer, Julius Benedict. The three-act opera is based on Dion Boucicault's popular play, The Colleen Bawn, also performed at the Palace.

The weekly Herald reported: "There was perhaps little required further than the announcement that the 'Lily of Killarney' was to be

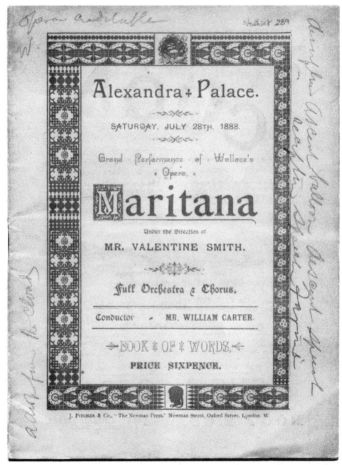

Maritana — Book of Words — © *The British Library Board. All rights reserved. Shelf mark: Northcott 289*

the programme of last Saturday evening, in order to secure a crowded and enthusiastic audience at the Alexandra Palace. Sir Julius Benedict's sparkling production occupies a highly favourable position amongst admirers of lyric drama."

Benedict is another of the handful of British-based composers of any note of the 19th century, but as with Balfe and Wallace, was not himself British. He was born in Stuttgart in 1804 to a family of bankers, and studied composition with Carl Maria von Weber, who introduced him to Beethoven. After stints in Vienna, Naples and Paris, he moved to London, where he spent the rest of his life.

He conducted at the Lyceum, Her Majesty's and Drury Lane and wrote operas, operettas, oratorios and a march for the wedding of the Prince of Wales. He was knighted in 1871, so came to Alexandra Palace with a considerable personal reputation, beside that of The Lily of Killarney.

The opera was first performed at Covent Garden in 1862 , but the Weekly Herald report suggests this production may have been based on a production in Liverpool, where Benedict conducted the Liverpool Philharmonic Society's concerts at the this time. The report also indicates the kind of adaptations that might be made to productions as they moved from venue to venue.

The Herald reported: "Though the text of Benedict's work — as first published, and produced by Carl Rosa — was by no means adhered to on Saturday, the greater part of several important scenes being cut out, the audience had ample opportunities of estimating both the merits of the opera and the abilities of the performers. The scenic effects and the general stage accessories were indeed replete, while the orchestra (conducted by Mr Ralph Horner) and chorus were characterised by their usual efficiency." Horner was the conductor of the D'Oyly Carte company at the time.

The cuts don't seem to have perturbed the audience, which gave ovations and encores. "Mr Ludwig's rendering of 'The Colleen Bawn, from childhood I have known' secured for him a second triumph and the number had to be repeated," the Herald reported.

Mr Ludwig also took a major part in the next opera, described by the Herald as the third of a series of nine Saturday night opera productions, and was clearly a regular and recognised performer at the Alexandra Palace Theatre. "Mr Ludwig is a universal favourite with the patrons of the Palace operas," the Herald said in its critique of Gounod's Faust, "and his appearance upon the stage in the character of Valentine was the signal for general applause."

Marguerite was played by an already successful soprano, Blanche Cole. She first performed as a child and made her first opera appearances in Fra Diavolo and La Sonnambula while still in her teens. She performed variously with the Carl Rosa Company, Richard Temple and Rose Hersee's company, as well as presenting her own company from time to time — as she would do later in November 1979, with La Sonnumbula at the Alexandra Palace Theatre.

She died of "dropsy" — probably congestive heart failure — at only 37 in 1888. One obituary commented: "She was everywhere known for her graceful acting, which, apart even from the careful manipulation of her pure and beautiful voice, made her a favourite with opera-goers."

The rest of the series included Weber's Der Freishutz, La Fille de Madame Angot ("the house was crowded in every part") and Auber's The Crown Diamonds, concluding in early June with George Macfarren's Robin Hood, with regulars including Blanche Cole, Aynsley Cook and Mr Ludwig.

Macfarren is also one of the few British-based composers of any note during the century and along with Arthur Sullivan the only true Brit, born in London, probably of Scottish parents. He trained at the Royal Academy of Music and concentrated on composition because of failing eyesight — he eventually went completely blind. Even so, he was to become a pillar of the musical establishment: head of the Royal Academy of Music, professor of music at Cambridge University and founder of the Handel Society.

According to the classical music label Naxos, which has released a modern recording of Robin Hood: "George Macfarren was considered by many of his contemporaries as the greatest British dramatic opera composer since Purcell"; adding that his roster of operas was "notable for its fine ensemble scenes, witty motifs, and deft, imaginative orchestrations".

Some contemporaries were less kind, one dismissing him as "essentially a musical grammarian". But he also had distinguished admirers. His Chevy Chase overture was performed by the Leipzig Gewandhaus Orchestra under Felix Mendelssohn and was admired by Richard Wagner — though Wagner also described Macfarren as "a pompous and melancholy Scot".

Robin Hood was "capitally put on the stage" at Alexandra Palace, according to the Weekly Herald which added: "We overheard many expressions of regret that this was the last opera of the series; and certainly nothing has been more lastingly popular at our Northern palace than the Saturday evening operas."

August saw the first performance, so far as we know, of a Gilbert and Sullivan opera at Alexandra Palace. HMS Pinafore was performed as a benefit in aid of the Metropolitan and City Police Orphanage.

In November, Blanche Cole's company performed La Sonnambula, but Carrington also lists four other operas performed that year, for which we have no further details: La Traviata (Verdi), Cinderella (Rossini), and Satanella, and The Puritan's Daughter (both by Balfe).

Also in November, the manager WH Jones applied to Edmonton Petty Sessions for a renewal of the theatre licence. When asked if they were ordinary plays that were performed, Jones replied "principally operas". After one Inspector Bullock offered the assurance that "recent trouble arising out of the races" did not extend to theatrical performances, the licence was renewed "providing that the plays shall be conducted with order and decency".

With a temporary lessee for just six months from May 1880, the theatre programme appears sparse, with only one opera of which we have any reports: Balfe's The Sleeping Queen, with Richard Temple in the cast and possibly the producer.

At the end of 1880, new lessees — WH Jones and the former catering manager Mr B Barber — took on the Palace. They concentrated their efforts on a big Easter opening for the summer season. There was a significant programme in the theatre of both plays and operas between Easter and Whitsun. Opera productions continued on through into June and August.

The Weekly Herald for 27 May 1881 reported: "The success of the Italian and English operas recently given at the Alexandra Palace under the musical conduct of Herr Meyer Lutz has justified the commencement of a series of English operas, extending over successive Saturdays during the summer, and produced under the stage direction of Mr Friend."

One of those preceding operas, perhaps sung in Italian, may have been Rossini's Barber of Seville, referred to by Carrington, but for which we have no reports. The first production of the Friend-Lutz regime was Donizetti's Lucia di Lammermoor, which attracted a "tolerably large audience … despite the counter attractions of a popular concert announced for the same evening on a platform overlooking the gorgeously illuminated triple lakes". Kenwood eat your heart out.

The report says that "A company well associated with the recent history of English opera has been secured", but it is not clear if this refers to Carl Rosa. Blanche Cole took the part of Lucia, with Fred Packard as Edgar, and new names such as James Sauvage and Dudley Thomas.

"Mr Packard," the Herald reported, "invested the part with considerable interest. In the duet with Lucia in the first act, 'My sighs shall on the balmy breeze', he broke slightly at a critical passage, but with this exception the performance was highly credible and the success was emphasised by repeated applause." Interesting to know how many local papers today would be able to display such keen critical perception of opera.

Packard sang the lead in Faust at the next Saturday night performance, with James Sauvage as Valentine and Alice Aynsley Cook as Siebel. An AP daily programme of events was annotated and seems to indicate that Annette Alba took the part of Marguerite, originally slated for Blanche Cole.

Alba also appears to have taken the lead role in Mayerbeer's Dinorah the following week. The cast also included Sauvage, Thomas and Alice Aynsley Cook — but also the most famous member of the Cook family, (John) Furneaux Cook. Furneaux Cook joined the D'Oyly Carte touring company in 1878 and played many of the baritone roles in Gilbert and Sullivan operas. He went on the D'Oyly Carte tour of America in 1879-80, but left on his return to England, only rejoining the company at the end of 1881.

Dinorah was followed a week later by Offenbach's Genevieve de Brabant.

August Bank Holiday saw an opera double bill, with Gilbert and Sullivan's Trial By Jury, with a cast including George Mudie, Henry Hallam and Juliette Piemonte; and The Waterman, an 18th-century English opera by Charles Dibden, with a cast including Mudie, Hallam, Piemonte and Sam Wilkinson, who was also to turn up as Dame Noodle in the pantomime Hop o' my Thumb later in the year.

In October, Emily Soldene appeared as Carmen in her own company's production of Bizet's opera. Also in the cast were Rose Lee, Richard Temple and Mr H Nordblom, "who is always a favourite here". The Weekly Herald reported that so successful was the performance and so enthusiastic the applause that "by request, the management announced that the opera would be repeated next Saturday". Perhaps also filling a gap in the programming.

Finally, on 27 December, Blanche Cole returned in Donizetti's comic opera, Elixir of Love (presumably an English-language version) — stage managed by the ever dependable TH Friend and conducted by Isidore di Solla.

Information for 1882 is sketchy at the moment. Carrington refers to a season of operas before Easter by "principals" from the Carl Rosa Company, including Maritana, La Sonnambula, Il Trovatore, The Bohemian Girl,

Lily of Killarney and Mozart's Don Giovanni, and Marriage of Figaro.

The AP programme of events for 29 April, lists Billee Taylor, a contemporary opera by Edward Solomon, premiered at the Imperial Theatre the previous October and at Alexandra Palace performed with a "powerful chorus and increased band, under the personal direction of the composer". The cast included the original Sir Mincing Lane — Arthur Williams — Philip Day as Billee and Emma Chambers as Arabella Lane.

But the financial clouds were gathering again. Jones and Barber petitioned for liquidation and the Palace would close for much of the next five years. Carrington records single performances of operas in 1887, including The Bohemian Girl, Il Trovatore, Faust, Don Giovanni and Beethoven's Fidelio.

1888 would be a swan song, with Valentine Smith from the Drury Lane Theatre mounting a last season of occasional opera performances. From July through to late October, there were performances of Maritana, Il Trovatore, The Bohemian Girl and La Sonnambula.

Maritana appears to have been performed at the end of July, then again at the end of August. One newspaper reported: "The introduction of opera at the Palace is a bold venture, but it will undoubtedly be successful if Wallace's grand romantic opera Maritana, under the direction of Mr Valentine Smith, of Drury Lane Theatre, as produced a crowded house last Saturday … can be considered a precedent."

"Miss Emily Parkinson as Maritana sang very sweetly indeed"; "Mr Valentine Smith as Don Caesar was superb, his voice always in tune and full of rich, soft melody"; "The chorus was exceptionally fine and too much praise cannot be accorded to the orchestra under the masterly directorship of Mr William Carter."

The performance of The Bohemian Girl on Thursday 13 September — possibly a special holiday — seems to have been helped by the general day out at the Palace. The Southwark Standard reported: "On Thursday, this now most popular place of amusement on the north side of London, was visited by upwards of 65,000 persons. The great attraction being the occasion of the 'King of Cloundlands' [Professor Baldwin, the balloonist] benefit, who it was announced would ascend and dive from an altitude of two miles."

The opera also soared, being declared "a decided success. The old and favourite songs being vociferously encored." Another performance of Maritana followed, where Valentine Smith as Don Caesar "brought down the house ever and anon, in tremendous applause".

The same report continued: "There has certainly in the history of the Palace never been a manager of the theatre who has been more popular; and if he has not achieved financial success he has most certainly deserved it."

This suggests perhaps that Smith had taken on the role which previously seems to have been carried out by Mr Friend. But it also sums up the problem of the Palace. On Thursday 18 October, a Grand Ballad concert was held in the theatre with many of the regular performers, including Smith, Grace Digby and Egbert Roberts. Another performance of Maritana took place on the Saturday, and then the fat lady sang and it was over. In early 1889 the Palace was closed to the public. Opera would not be sung in the Theatre again until the new century.

Drama at the Palace

From our current research we can identify over 60 productions of plays at the Alexandra Palace Theatre. Just under half would count as what we might call serious or straight spoken drama, increasingly popular with a growing middle-class audience, and the rest farces, which were largely taking over from the earlier burlesques and were more likely to appeal to a more popular audience.

Many dramas would also have included elements of music and spectacle, and would often have been programmed within a wider day's entertainment. The first major day of the second Palace, Whit Monday 1875, is typical, with the programme in the Theatre beginning with an operetta, The Elfin Tree, followed by the first performance of the spectacle Minerva, followed by a farce, The Area Belle, then a second performance of Minerva.

In terms of repertoire, the most performed writer, from the productions we currently know of, was the popular Victorian playwright Dion Boucicault, with seven plays performed (Rip Van Winkle, The Colleen Bawn, London Assurance, The Flying Scud, Led Astray, Streets of London and The Shaughran). He is followed by Shakespeare (Hamlet, Othello, As You Like It and The Merchant of Venice) and Tom Taylor (Our American Cousin, Henry Dunbar and Twixt Axe and Crown, Nine Points of the Law) with four each; WS Gilbert with three plays performed (Creatures of Impulse, Pygmalion and Galatea, and Sweethearts); followed by Sheridan (School for Scandal, The Rivals); GR Sims (Crutch and Toothpick, The Member for Slocum); and James Albery (Where's the Cat?, Pink Dominoes) with two apiece.

Some of the most popular Victorian melodramas were also performed, including the theatrical version of Elizabeth Braddon's Lady Audley's Secret (performed as a play-reading in the newly accessed auditorium in 2004), Ellen Wood's East Lynne ("Gone, and never called me mother"), and Peril, Scott and Stephenson's adaptation of Victorien Sardou's Nos Intimes, performed at the Palace, according to Carrington, by two of the greatest actors of the age, Henry Beerbohm Tree and Lily Langtree.

It is likely that most, if not all, were productions transferred from other theatres or were touring productions. Although the evidence is sketchy, credits for several theatre companies are noted in programmes and reviews, including the Strand Theatre Company, Mr Swanborough's Company, Wyndham's, and Harry Paulton's company. Charles Kelly, the estranged husband of Ellen Terry, also appears to have brought two Shakespeare productions to the theatre in 1881.

The first two performances for which we have details were both farces, though they brought some illustrious names to the Palace. By the 1870s, farce seems to have largely replaced burlesque as the most popular form of broad theatrical entertainment. But with their exaggerated and improbable situations and often incomprehensible plots, physical humour, deliberate nonsense and stylised acting, they remain in the tradition that stretches back through burlesque to the Harlequinade and Commedia dell'Arte.

Farces remained part of the dramatic fare until the late 20th century, but with the end of Brian Rix's Whitehall farces and Ray Clooney's productions, as a genre they have mainly disappeared, though playwrights such as Alan Ayckbourn may still use the form. It still survives on TV, perhaps, in programmes such as Mrs Brown's Boys and various offerings by Vic Reeves and Bob Mortimer.

The Area Belle was written by William Brough and Andrew Halliday, both journalists turned stage writers. Brough we have met before as the writer of the pantomime, Turko the Terrible. Andrew Halliday was a Scot who contributed to Henry Mayhew's ground-breaking study of Victorian life, London Labour and the London Poor, and wrote for Charles Dickens's magazine All Year Round. His most successful theatrical piece was probably Little Em'ly, an adaptation of Dickens' David Copperfield, which gained the approval of the author.

Brough and Halliday co-authored several farces in the 1860s, including The Area Belle. The plot concerns a love tussle over Penelope, the Area Belle, between the policeman Pitcher and the guardsman Tosser. (The latter part was on a later occasion apparently played by Baden Powell, the founder of the scouts, but it is not recorded what kind of a Tosser he was.)

At Alexandra Palace, Pitcher was played by Frederick Sullivan (the brother of composer Arthur Sullivan), who just months before had created the role of the Learned Judge in Gilbert and Sullivan's Trial by Jury. The writer FC Burnand called him "one of the most naturally comic little men I ever came across". As Sullivan was then appearing in productions at the Royalty Theatre, it may well be that this was a production from that theatre.

In June, another notable actor appeared at Alexandra Palace in a play which has gone down in history — though not for its dramatic qualities. The actor Edward Askew Sothern reprised one of the classic roles of late Victorian theatre, Lord Dundreary in Tom Taylor's Our American Cousin.

Tom Taylor was almost a caricature of the Victorian polymath: a journalist who became editor of Punch, art critic of the Times, for two years professor of English at University College, a lawyer at Middle Temple and an assistant secretary of the Board of Health. In between times — whenever that was — he turned out about 100 plays, many adaptations from the French or in collaboration, including The Ticket of Leave Man and Twixt Axe and Crown, the latter also produced at Alexandra Palace.

Our American Cousin premiered in New York in 1858. Dundreary was initially a minor part, which Sothern hesitated about taking, bringing the riposte from the lead actor Joseph Jefferson, that "there are no small parts, only small actors" — a sentiment paraphrased most notably, perhaps, in the film Sunset Boulevard. Sothern began playing Dundreary as a lisping fop and added gags and physical humour until it became virtually the central figure in the play — and one much repeated and copied.

Taylor's plays are now largely forgotten, except for one performance of Our American Cousin in April 1865. Halfway through act III scene 2 at Ford's Theatre in Washington, during the laughter that followed one of the funniest lines in the play, from the actor Harry Hawk playing the title role, another actor, John Wilkes Booth, added his own dramatic touch by fatally shooting President Abraham Lincoln.

No such dramatic interventions occurred at Alexandra Palace, so far as is known. The summer of 1875 brought some more traditional theatre fare: productions of Richard Brinsley Sheridan's The School for Scandal, and The Rivals; and Oliver Goldsmith's She Stoops to Conquer; along with a now less known 18th-century comedy, George Coleman's The Jealous Wife.

According to the Weekly Herald, the principal characters of She Stoops to Conquer were "represented by some of the first artistes of the day". It added: "The large theatre was well filled on the occasion and the performance passed off with éclat."

The School for Scandal included the well-known actress Jane Vezin, born in England but raised to become a child prodigy in Australia, before returning in 1857 to a distinguished career on the London stage. In her first season at Sadler's Wells Theatre she played several Shakespearian leading ladies, as well as Lydia Languish in The Rivals

Daily Programme, including Led Astray — Courtesy of Bruce Castle Museum (Haringey Culture, Libraries and Learning)

and Mrs Oakley in The Jealous Wife. A decade later at Drury Lane, she also played Lady Teazle in School for Scandal, so she may have appeared in all this summer season at Alexandra Palace. Indeed, she had toured with her own company the previous year. Unfortunately, we have at the moment no further information on the productions to clarify this.

Equally adept at comedy or serious drama, her own life ended in tragedy when she threw herself out of a bedroom window after the death of her daughter in 1901.

The summer season ended with more farces around the bank holiday at the end of August, including Raising the Wind, The Two Orphans, and Paul Meritt's Chopstick and Spikins, in which "Mr George Conquest amused a large audience by his personation of Samuel Spikins". The popular Chopsticks and Spikins returned the following year.

The dust of history has settled on Raising the Wind, but The Two Orphans appears to be (yet another) adaptation of a French play, Les Deux Orphelines by Adolphe D'Ennery and Eugene Cormon, a melodrama about two homeless orphans separated when one is kidnapped. It was twice made into a film, in 1915 with Theda Bara, and in 1921 by DW Griffith, starring Dorothy and Lillian Gish. But its main claim to fame is its starring role in yet another historical tragedy: it was being performed the night of the Brooklyn Theatre fire of 1876, in which around 300 people lost their lives.

George Conquest also made an appearance at a patriotic "fete and banquet" in commemoration of the Charge of the Light Brigade — though the inclusion of two farces and Offenbach's opera-bouffe The Brigands, suggests it was not an entirely tearful event. The dramatic performances were interspersed with renditions of Tennyson's famous poem, and other recitals and musical interludes.

Raising the Wind was again performed in this programme, according to the credits, by the Strand Theatre Company by permission of Mrs Swanborough. The Swanboroughs were largely female Victorian theatrical dynasty, with both Louisa and Ada Swanborough taking leading roles as actresses. But Louisa was also a licensee of the Strand Theatre, as was Mary Ann, who appears to have been licensee there at the time of this performance.

The second farce, Brother Bill and Me, is by William E Suter, with contributions by the comic actor, Arthur Williams. Suter is perhaps best known for his adaptation of Elizabeth Mary Braddon's Lady Audley's Secret, a play which was to be performed at Alexandra Palace in May of the next year. However, it is not known if it was his version of the Braddon book or that of CH Hazlewood which was performed.

Lady Audley's Secret is a key work in popular Victorian literature. Mary Elizabeth Braddon's novel, which made both her and her publisher rich — he built a villa in Barnes and named it Audley Lodge — was the most successful of the so-called sensation novels. It was inspired by the story of Constance Kent, who was accused of an infamous 1860 child murder which obsessed the Victorians and has had an impact down to today. Wilkie Collins included elements of the story in The Moonstone and Kate Summerscale revisited the case in her 2008 book The Suspicions of Mr Whicher.

In the Kent case, a body of a young boy was found in an outside privy. In Lady Audley, a husband is pushed down a well. As in the Kent case, Braddon's novel raises issues that were increasingly causing Victorian middle-class anxieties. Lady Audley is a bigamist, able to hide her identity because growing urbanisation gives people anonymity; the sanctity of the idealised domestic realm seems to be threatened by social change; and class distinctions are becoming eroded. Madness is also a theme, frequently being ascribed to women who seek to control their own lives.

In Lady Audley, the protagonist is a governess who marries an ageing well-off landowner, Sir Michael Audley. But she is already married, her husband having left for Australia to pan for gold. On his unexpected return, he visits Audley End with his old friend, Robert Audley, Sir Michael's nephew. Lady Audley has to avoid her husband, who then disappears — as it later transpires pushed down the well (though he survives, returning to Australia). When Robert discovers Lady Audley's Secret, she tries to set fire to the inn where he is staying and ends up being committed to a mental institution.

No doubt its themes of urbanisation, class anxiety and arson would have resonated at Alexandra Palace, but regrettably we have at the moment no further details of the production or its reception there.

Lady Audley was preceded in May 1876 by a production of Rip Van Winkle. American writer Washington Irving's short story of 1819 has been widely adapted to other media, with its lovable but lazy character in pre-revolutionary New York, who drinks moonshine and wakes up after the revolution is over. It was adapted for the stage by Dion Boucicault for the actor Joseph Jefferson, of Our American Cousin fame, and the Weekly Herald suggests that Jefferson played the character of Rip Van Winkle at the Palace.

Dion Boucicault's work features prominently at the Alexandra Palace Theatre over the next couple of years. Despite the vast numbers of plays produced in the mid-Victorian era, Boucicault is perhaps the only dramatist of lasting significance between Sheridan at the beginning of the century and the late Victorians such as Pinero, Wilde and Shaw. And even his reputation rests today largely on one play written in

1841 when he was just 19. There is a possibility that London Assurance may have been performed at the Palace in 1876, but it was certainly performed in 1882.

The Colleen Bawn, performed at the Alexandra Palace Theatre in June 1876, and "which drew forth tremendous applause", was Boucicault's most popular play, performed in all the main cities of both Britain and the US. It made him a fortune, largely lost in theatre management in London. The play was written at the end of Boucicault's first stay in New York, from 1854-60 and first produced there. Its mix of financial hardship, hidden marriages and foiled murder plots in rural Ireland fits the melodrama mould of Lady Audley's Secret.

Indeed, life would mimic art at the end of his life. On a tour of Australia in 1885, Boucicault left his wife to marry a young actress of 20, having his first marriage finally dissolved in 1888 on the grounds of bigamy and adultery.

The Colleen Bawn was also turned into an opera by Sir Jules Benedict which was also produced at Alexandra Palace.

The next year, The Colleen Bawn was produced twice in the summer season at Alexandra Palace, in June and August 1877. The June performance was most notable for the visit to the Palace by the former US president and civil war general, Ulysses S Grant, though it appears he did not risk visiting the Theatre.

Again, the season opened in May with Boucicault's version of Rip Van Winkle, though the Weekly Herald damned it with faint praise. The production of Rip Van Winkle, it noted, was transferred to the Palace Theatre under the direction of John Hollingshead.

It then continued: "The theatre was crowded, and the audience, evidently disposed to be both pleased and patient, sat the representation out, occasionally rewarding the chief characters with sparse applause. Several ... blunders in the stage business were overlooked and the interspersion of the dialogue with some capital puns tended to give the performance, as a whole, a passable effect."

The stage "business" is the term that was used to describe the scene shifting and other technical operations and effects. That there were blunders in this production may indicate that some of these productions came in with little rehearsal time to accommodate the production to the Alexandra Palace Theatre's stage.

Hollingshead's CV bears similarities to Andrew Halliday's. Born in London's East End, he started his working life as a bookkeeper for a clothing company, but showed he had other ambitions by writing essays on social reform. He set up a penny paper with a friend and in the mid-1850s became a full-time writer, starting as journalist on Charles Dickens's Household Words magazine. He then moved to equally illustrious company, under WM Thackeray at his Cornhill Magazine.

Later in life he returned to writing, mainly about the theatre, but in the 1860s he became a theatre impresario, first at the Alhambra Theatre and in 1868 at the Gaiety, which specialised in burlesque, variety, light opera and comedy. Most famously, he brought together Gilbert and Sullivan to produce a musical extravaganza, Thespis, which kicked off the most celebrated theatrical collaboration of the age. Several names associated with the Gaiety were also linked to Alexandra Palace, including Edward Kelly, Kate Vaughan and the musical director Meyer Lutz.

July 1877 saw the production of another Boucicault play, The Flying Scud, a racing drama with a full cast augmented, according to an AP programme of events, by "jockeys, stable lads, trainers, touts, showmen, policemen etc". Racing plays were produced in the late Victorian era, with various ways of presenting the races, including using a treadmill in later Victorian productions.

The bank holiday programme on 6 August consisted of two performances of a "musical absurdity" called Crazed by Alfred Phillips, featuring a mad composer called Beethoven Brown; with a "laughable, protean sketch", Day After The Fair, based, it seems, on a Thomas Hardy short story, in between. Loosely based, presumably, as it included during the performance, the song Buy A Box Of Lights, a banjo solo and dance.

The evening was rounded off with another performance of The Colleen Bawn, produced by "Mr Swanborough's company", before a full house.

Easter 1878, with a change of management, saw the summer season at the Palace open with a more populist programme. Easter Monday had a variety programme, including the Gaiety Theatre burlesque Little Doctor Faust, directed by John Hollingshead, and with the "specially engaged" Edward Terry as Mephistopheles.

Edward O'Connor Terry was a hugely influential Victorian theatrical figure. He was said to be the illegitimate son of the Irish Chartist leader, Feargus O'Connor, and later in life would himself be a leading figure in another semi-clandestine organisation, the Freemasons — which probably included a number of other theatrical figures.

He began his career in the theatre in the 1860s in the provinces with a young Henry Irving, becoming successful in comedy at the Royal Strand Theatre. But he reached the height of his success and fame in

the Gaiety Theatre burlesques from 1876 on. He went into management in the 1880s, opening Terry's Theatre on the Strand, where he
appeared to great success in the plays of Arthur Wing Pinero. His
second wife was Lady Florence Harris, the widow of the impresario
Augustus Harris, emphasising, perhaps, the informal freemasonry of
the Victorian theatre.

Terry also took the lead role in John Poole's 1825 farce Paul Pry on
another variety-based programme at the end of May 1878 at Alexandra
Palace.

In June and July there was more serious drama on offer, with a
production of Boucicault's Led Astray — another adaptation from a
French play, La Tentation — which gives one of the first Alexandra
Palace credits for Mr TH Friend, as stage manager. The AP programme
of events records this as a Saturday matinee performance on Whit weekend, with the Theatre again being given over to variety on the Monday.

The AP programme also records a performance of Hamlet at the
end of June — again a matinee, preceded, it seems, by a performance
of part of Beethoven's Egmont overture — perhaps an indication that
even Shakespeare needed some adornment for the Theatre's regular
audience. It seems a short engagement for an orchestra, so perhaps
there were more musical interludes. Incidental music was played at
some spoken drama performances in Victorian theatres, perhaps the
origins of its use in cinema.

Hamlet and Ophelia were played by Mr and Mrs Bandmann, the
latter "by permission of FB Chatterton", who ran the Theatre Royal
Drury Lane, so the production may have been a spin off from there.
Daniel Bandmann was a German-American, mainly Shakespearian
actor who appeared on the British stage in the late 1860s and 1870s.
He toured extensively throughout Britain, Australia, New Zealand
and North America, publishing in 1886 An Actor's Tour or Seventy
Thousand Miles with Shakespeare. He ended life as a Montana rancher,
unable to handle being tied down maybe.

Millicent Palmer-Bandmann, not only played Ophelia. She also
made a name for herself playing Hamlet as a leading "travesti" actor
— principal boys were not just a pantomime custom in the less rigidly
segmented Victorian theatre.

The Rivals in July 1878 was directed by TH Friend, with Captain
Absolute played by Harold Kyrle Money Bellew, who made a career
playing romantic comedy roles. Kyrle went to Australia in his late teens
and became a journalist before being seduced by the theatre, against

colleagues' advice, and returning to Britain in 1875. In the 1880s he was associated with Henry Irving, and later Wallacks Theatre in New York. The Australian Dictionary of National Biography describes his manner as "ingratiating, his voice penetrating and pleasant, his style forcible and picturesque".

At the end of July, there was a production of WJ Wills's historical drama, Nell Gwynne, which had debuted at the Royalty Theatre a few months earlier. Wills was an Irish dramatist and Bohemian, whose main interest was oil painting. "His plays were a by-product, in which he took little interest after he had furnished the manuscript," according to his OUP biography. Which is why he is probably best remembered for his oil-painting of Ophelia which hung at the Lyceum Theatre for many years.

The 1878 season ended in more spectacular fashion. The AP programme advertises for 8 August a "Grand Military Spectacle" in the Theatre by the Canterbury Hall Company, under the direction of E Villiers. Seats were advertised for this piece of contemporary political theatre at sixpence and one shilling, with "A few stalls, 2s 6d, to which season ticket holders may pass with 1s tickets".

Plevna brings together several strands of Victorian popular culture. The five-month siege of the Ottoman fortress of Plevna in modern Bulgaria by Russian and Romanian forces from July to December 1877 struck a similar chord in the public imagination as the Charge of the Light Brigade in the Crimean war (commemorated by performances in the Alexandra Palace Theatre and a banquet in 1875). Approaching the peak of British global and imperial power, Boy's Own adventures of military derring-do found a ready audience.

History would later see the siege as part of a war of liberation by the peoples of eastern Europe from Turkish rule. But in a climate of continued fears about growing Russian power, the outnumbered Ottoman defenders of Plevna became popular heroes, as newspapers all over Europe carried detailed reports of the siege.

According to the programme of events: "This entertainment consists of a Panorama of the Seat of War, from Constantinople to the scenes of chief interest, with a diorama of Plevna and representation by several hundred boys" (maybe part of the reason for the Theatre's later censure by the Tottenham school board for its use of under-age performers).

It continues: "The views and costumes from sketches taken by Mr F Villiers, the special correspondent and artist, who visited every town and city given in the panorama … presented to the public by kind permission of the proprietors of The Graphic."

Frederic Villiers had just left art school at the Royal Academy when the rebellion in eastern Europe began with a declaration of war by Serbia on Turkey in 1876. Then in his mid-twenties, Villiers approached The Graphic newspaper to work as a war artist covering the conflict. It was

Alexandra Palace Daily Programme.

The ORCHESTRAL BAND will perform Beethoven's "Egmont" Overture before the Tragedy (2.50).

Three o'clock, in the Theatre,
Reserved Seats, 6d. and 1s.　Stalls, 2s. 6d.
SHAKESPEARE'S TRAGEDY,

"HAMLET."

Hamlet	Mr. BANDMANN.
Claudius (King of Denmark)	Mr. BURNE.
Polonius (Lord Chamberlain)	Mr. W. H. STEPHENS.

(By permission of C. Mortimer, Esq.)

Horatio	Mr. OUTRAM.
Laertes	Mr. W. REDMUND.

(By permission of C. Mortimer, Esq.)

Marcellus	Mr. HINTON.
First Actor	Mr. DAVID EVANS.

(By permission of C. Mortimer, Esq.)

Second Actor	Mr. HEARDWICK.
First Gravedigger	Mr. ARTHUR WILLIAMS.

(By permission of W. Holland, Esq.)

Second Gravedigger	Mr. WATSON.
Bernardo	Mr. BRUTON.
Francisco	Mr. HEARD.
Ghost	Mr. E. F. EDGAR.
Actress	Miss BEUSTON.

AND

Ophelia	Mrs. BANDMANN.

(By permission of F. B. Chatterton, Esq.)

Lords, Ladies, Officers, Soldiers, Sailors, Messengers, and Attendants.

Quarter to Seven, in the Central Hall,

THE GREAT CIRCUS.

Mr. Wieland's Entirely New Company,
Including Marie Ashby and Sam Watson.
Reserved Seats, 6d. and 1s.
(For Programme see previous announcement.)

Quarter-past Seven,
MARAZ and DEZMON
In New Startling Feats on the High Bars; after which

MARAZ.

The Aerial Diver, will descend in a rapid eagle-like swoop from the roof to the floor of the Great Central Hall.

Eight o'clock, in the Central Hall,

PROMENADE CONCERT.

1. OVERTURE, "Guillaume Tell"		*Rossini.*
Solos for Cello, Herr A. BOUMAN; Cor. Anglais, Mr. MAISCH; Flute, Mr. HIBB.		
2. BOAT SONG, "Hail to the Chief"		*Sir H. Bishop.*
ALEXANDRA PALACE CHOIR.		
3. MINUETTO & TRIO (Symphony in G minor)		*W. N. Bennett.*
4. SCENA, "C'era una volta, mi principe"		*C. Gounod.*
Mdlle. Lino.		
5. BALLET MUSIC, "Romeo e Giulietta"		*Gounod.*
6. PART SONG, "Departure"		*Mendelssohn.*
THE ALEXANDRA PALACE CHOIR.		
7. NEW VALSE, "The Belles of Dublin" (first time)		*Frederic Archer*
8. JEWEL SONG (Faust)		*Gounod.*
Mdlle. Lino.		
9. MARCH AND CHORUS, "Tannhäuser"		*Wagner.*

Director of the Music, Mr. FREDERIC ARCHER.

Half-past Nine,

Grand Display of Fireworks,

BY MR. JAMES PAIN.

A few Reserved Seats for Fireworks, 2s. 6d. and 1s.
Entrance from South-west Corridor opposite Italian Garden.

1. Aerial Maroons.
2. Illumination of South Park and Race Course.
3. Discharge of Large Bouquet Rockets.
4. Ascent of Balloons, carrying Magnesium Lights and other pleasing Fireworks.
5. Aladdin's Jewelled Trees.
6. Flight of Shells Golden Cloud.
7. Swarms of Brilliant Snakes.
8. Asteroids with Four Floating Lights.
9. Asteroids with Eight Floating Lights.
10. Asteroids with Silver Star and Bouquets.

11. Mammoth Silver Fire Wheels with newly devised intersecting Centres Banked on either side with Illuminated Danish Devices (first time).
12. Aerial Candescent.
13. Eight-inch Shells.
14. Tourbillions in Gold and Silver Fires.
15. Great Set Piece a propos to the Berlin Congress. Fire Portraits of 1. The Earl of Beaconsfield. 2. Prince Gortchakow. 3. Prince Bismarck. 4. Mehemet Ali Pasha. 5. Count Andrassy.
16. Flight of Shells, forming Golden Clouds studded with Jewels.
17. Great Cascade of Golden Fire, surmounted by Batteries of Roman Candles.
18. Salvo of 12-inch Shells.
19. Flight of Rockets forming a gigantic and magnificent Aerial Bouquet.

During the Fireworks,
THE PALACE MILITARY BAND
(Conductor, Mr. JANSSENS), will perform.

Finale,
Organ Performance by Mr. Archer

THE SWIMMING BATH

(NEAR WOOD GREEN ENTRANCE)
Now Open for the Season, under the management of PROFESSOR BECKWITH.

Admission 6d., Season Tickets, 10s.; to Youths and Schools, 7s. 6d.
The Bath and the Wood Green and Hornsey Entrances are open from 6 a.m. daily.
Ladies taught Swimming twice a week by Miss BECKWITH, on Tuesdays and Thursdays from 11 till 4.

THE BILLIARD SALOON

(Near the Reading Room)
IS NOW OPEN under the management of Mr. G. COLLINS, winner of the First Prize in the Great American Tournament held in London in February last. Lessons given daily. Several important Matches will take place during the season.

THE DENAYROUZE DIVING PAVILION

Is close to the East entrance to the Palace, and is it throughout the day Divers will give Practical Illustrations of the use of the most improved Diving Appliances, speaking Apparatus, Submarine Lamps, &c., in an Enormous Tank, containing nearly 40 Tons of Water. Divers can be seen at work, and conversed with by Visitors. Under the direction of Mr. R. APPLEGARTH. Admission Threepence.

CAPTAIN FROOMBERG'S
INDIAN SNAKE CHARMERS & CONJURORS
In LONDESBOROUGH ROOM, at intervals during the day.

BALDWIN'S WORKING BEES

are located at the back of the Great Orchestra, First Floor.
Admission Threepence.

Boating, Canoeing, Swings, Roundabouts, Archery, Rifle Shooting at 100 yards (near the first of the Triple Lakes), Gymnasium, Cosmorama, Camera Obscura (near the Great Lake), the new Monkey House (close to Conservatory at West Entrance), &c.

THE FOLLOWING SPECIAL TRAINS

will leave the High Level Station This Evening.
8.15　To Finsbury Park and King's Cross.
8.45　To Finsbury Park and Broad Street.
9.15　To Finsbury Park and King's Cross.
9.45　To Finsbury Park and Broad Street.
And every few minutes after Ten o'clock.

REFRESHMENT DEPARTMENT,

ON SOUTH SIDE OF THE PALACE.
In the Dining Saloon (in the Corridor near the Bazaar)—
Hot Dinners à la Carte from 2s. 6d. to 7s. 6d.
In the Dining Saloon (in the Corridor near the Bazaar)—
Cold Dinners, 2s. and 3s. Tea, 1s. 6d.
In the Tea Room (in the Corridor near the Italian Garden)—
Luncheons, Tea and Coffee, and Light Refreshments, as per Tariff.
Private Dining Rooms may be engaged on application at the office of the Refreshment Department, Corridor near the Bazaar.

A SWIMMING CLUB of Gentlemen Amateurs
is being formed in connection with the Swimming Bath. Gentlemen wishing to join should apply to Mr. W. Beckwith, at the Bath.

THE WHITEHALL REVIEW; a Weekly Journal of Politics, Finance, and Society, with Crayon Portrait.
Price Sixpence.

Daily Programme, including Hamlet — Courtesy of Bruce Castle Museum (Haringey Culture, Libraries and Learning)

the start of a long career in which he covered not only later wars in the Balkans and eastern Europe, but British imperial wars in Egypt, Afghanistan and Sudan.

Canterbury Hall, just south of the river in Lambeth, where the spectacle was first conceived and performed, plays a key role in the history of the music hall. The first Canterbury Hall, seating 700, was built in 1852 as an adjunct to a public house, similar to other venues in the capital. Following its growing success, an enlarged 1,500-seat hall was built in 1856.

To keep the revenues flowing in, it was constructed around the existing hall and the original walls demolished over a weekend — an option unfortunately not available to Alexandra Palace after it burnt down in 1873. The Alexandra Palace Theatre has often been compared with Canterbury Hall because of its elongated auditorium, a design feature of music halls which seated the audience at tables where they could eat, smoke and drink.

Plevna was described by Canterbury Hall as a "popular ballet", one of a series choreographed by the Belgian Henri Leopold de Winne, to which the crowds flocked, including the Prince of Wales. The two leading dancers, Phyllis Broughton and Florence Powell, came with the company to Alexandra Palace.

These popular ballets were mounted by a new manager, Edwin Villiers — no relation to Frederic Villiers, as far as is known — who took over and enlarged the hall once again in 1876. Canterbury Hall was the venue for the first performances in Britain of Jacques Offenbach's operettas and in the early days often featured selections from operas — the singers attracted by the higher fees.

But popularity increased when classical music was dropped and the bills concentrated on the new working-class performers such as George Leybourne, "Champagne Charlie". It was rebuilt again in 1890 by Frank Matcham as the 3,000-seat Canterbury Theatre of Varieties. Charlie Chaplin appeared there as did his father before him.

The diorama was invented in the 1820s by the Frenchman Daguerre, a pioneer of photography. Scenes were painted on a series of linen panels with transparent sections, so that with changes in the lighting, different combinations of scenery could be seen and the scene would appear to change naturally. Often dioramas were in special buildings, but with advances in lighting — the originals used sunlight — they could be produced in ordinary theatres. Several were produced at the Alexandra Palace Theatre in the late 1890s, when licensing problems seems to have prevented live performance.

September 1878 at the Alexandra Palace Theatre featured another emblematic Victorian drama: Mazeppa. It's important both because

Mazeppa is one of the key artistic works of the 19th century — and because of its representation in a particular from of drama: hippodrama — quite literally drama with horses.

Mazeppa began its artistic life as a narrative poem by Lord Byron, published in 1819 and based on a popular legend about the early life of Ivan Mazepa, a Ukrainian who later became headman of the Cossacks. In the story, the young Mazeppa falls in love with Countess Theresa, a young woman married to an older aristocrat. On discovering the affair, the Count takes his revenge by tying Mazeppa naked to a wild horse which is then set free. The poem tells of the tribulations of Mazeppa during his wild ride.

Though apparently not considered highly by Byron scholars, it had enormous influence throughout the 19th century, particularly with the Romantics. Victor Hugo wrote his own poetic version of Mazeppa in 1829 and around the same time Alexander Pushkin wrote a narrative poem about a later incident in Mazepa's life as a rejoinder to Byron. Painters who have depicted Mazeppa's wild ride include Gericault and Delacroix.

Among other works based on the story are dramas by Juliusz Slowacki (1839) and FA Brady (1856), operas by Balfe, Tchaikovsky and Munchheimer, a symphonic poem by Lizst and a 1993 French film.

But it was perhaps most notable as one of the greatest examples of the strange (to modern eyes) hybrid oeuvre of hippodrama — for which it was, of course, ideally suited. According to AF Saxon, author of Enter Foot And Horse: A History Of Hippodrama of England and France: "The true hippodrama, as the name implies, is literally a play in which trained horses are considered as actors, with business, often leading actions, of their own to perform."

Horses first began to appear in theatres in the late 18th century, and developed out of equestrian circus. Hippodramas, with specially written plays, first began to appear in the early 1800s at venues such as Astley's Ampiheatre in London and the Cirque Olympique in Paris, where up to 36 riders could perform simultaneously. The hybrid form, with its mix of spectacle and melodrama, was particularly popular with the working classes, and venues combined a proscenium arch with a dirt-floored riding area in front of the orchestra pit, linked to the stage by ramps.

There was a particular impetus in Britain because of the restrictions of the Licensing Act, which restricted full performance of spoken drama to just two theatres in London. Philip Astley hit on a way that he could circumvent his licence for "public dancing and music ... and other entertainments of the kind". He realised that he could produce real drama — as long as it was performed on horseback. So he set about adapting well-known stories and plays.

Astley's financial success with The Blood Red Knight in 1810 persuaded reluctant managements at the patent theatres, Covent Garden and Drury Lane, to follow suit. An impetus to the form was given by the end of the Napoleonic wars in 1815, which left a ready supply of demobbed cavalry officers and trained horses. Mazeppa appears to have been first performed in England in 1823, but its major success was at Astley's Ampitheatre in 1831, becoming a worldwide success in the following decades.

Hippodrama was particularly popular in the United States, and was the most popular dramatic form throughout the 19th century in the western states — perhaps the model for Buffalo Bill's Wild West Show, which later appeared at the Alexandra Palace Theatre. Mazeppa, it seems, in the fashion of the day, was often played by a woman. A particularly notorious interpreter was the American actress Idah Isaacs Menken, who caused scandal when she appeared in an 1861 New York production tied to the horse wearing only a flesh coloured body-stocking.

Hippodrama hasn't entirely vanished. The Cavalla circus/performance company tours the world with shows featuring up to 30 horses, while in 2009 the O2 arena in London produced a one-off spectacular of Ben Hur, with over 30 horses and some 400 actors. In the later 19th century, hippodrama led to a wider use of all kinds of animals in the theatre, including dogs, monkeys, rabbits, donkeys and even elephants.

Unfortunately, we don't know if the version of Mazeppa produced at the Alexandra Palace was actually a hippodrama. It is described as a "romantic drama in three acts" and the plot description includes "Mazeppa bound to the wild horse of Tartary ... The wild horse pursued by Wolves ... Death of the wild horse ... Rescue of Mazeppa". The cast list refers to extras such as "Chieftains, Warriors, Priests, Shepherds etc" but makes no mention of any actual horses.

Maybe the "business" was achieved some other way — horse racing drama in the late Victorian period used props and treadmills. Mazeppa was played by Miss Lisa Weber, but we have no information on whether she caused scandal among the upright citizens of Muswell Hill. Interestingly — shades of Plevna — the third act concludes with a "Grand Military Ballet".

Both 1879 and 1880 were difficult years at the Palace and we have, at the moment, information on just one spoken drama in 1879 — operas were the mainstay that season — and five in 1880.

Round The Clock, performed in June 1879, was a "farcical absurdity" — again adapted from the French — by John F McArdle, a composer and lyricist. (One of his greatest successes was She's A Darling, She's A Dumpling, She's A Lamb.)

The summer of 1880 in the theatre seems to have been a mix of opera, dance and acrobatics, rounded off by the spectacle, The Triumph Of Summer. We currently have a record of one drama production in May (Little Doctor Faust again), two productions in August (a reprise for The Rivals and She Stoops To Conquer), and two in September.

The Liar is a two-act comedy written in 1762 by Samuel Foote, one of the major theatrical figures of the 18th century. Foote was the son of the honourable member of parliament for Tiverton and was himself honoured by being "disenrolled" from Oxford. At 20 he married for money — soon discarding the bride when his finances improved — but still ended up in debtor's prison. So he knew a bit about dissembling.

He then turned to the theatre under the tutelage of a major figure of the time, Charles Macklin, becoming successful as an actor. But still impoverished, he turned impresario, taking a lease on the Haymarket Theatre in 1746. He began also to write for the theatre, falling foul of the Licensing Act and entering into feuds with the writer Henry Fielding, the actor Henry Woodward, and the Methodists. In 1766 he lost a leg in a riding accident while riding with the Duke of York. Possibly, as a result, he received a patent for the Haymarket for a summer season of "legitimate" plays, probably the only amendment to the two patent theatres' monopoly.

It ended badly. In 1774, he himself was lampooned by one of his targets and accused of homosexuality (he was later acquitted of a legal charge). He was forced to give up his patent to another playwright, George Coleman (author of A Jealous Wife) in 1776, and died in transit to France the following year. His main legacy today is as author of the term "the grand panjamdrum". And, perhaps, his Bohemian lifestyle — which puts even some of his colourful Victorian successors in the shade.

The performance of The Liar at Alexandra Palace seems to have passed off without scandal, to the relief no doubt of the respectable operators of the Palace.

A few days later, a touring American Company, Salsbury's Troubadours, performed two theatrical entertainments, Love And Rain, followed by The Brook — which has been claimed by one source to

be the first American musical, that country's distinct contribution to
theatre, mixing ballad and comic opera, minstrelsy, and vaudeville —
"a combination of separate entertainments, or acts, with no plot, or
particular order".

Salsbury's troupe was formed in 1870s Chicago by Nate Salsbury,
who as producer, manager and writer, created farces for working-class
audiences. An Alexandra Palace daily programme of events for the
year describes the entertainments as "a novelty in the sense that it is
different in its motive and execution from any musical production of
its kind ... The musical morceaux and speciality efforts are suggested by
the situation that a party of actors and actresses would find themselves
in when dependent on each other for amusement.

"The matter of plot and incident find their location in the minds of
the spectators, who are thus cordially invited to share the general fun of
the evening, not as critics, but as parties to a jolly good time that shall
remind them of a similar past experience in their own lives."

The musical director was Charles Borgam and the songs included
The Song Of The Brook, The Lads Are Out Today, Love, Heartrending
Love, and Rain Rain Go Away — titles which would not be amiss in the
song list of a mid-20th-century musical (unlike, say, John F McArdle's
ditties).

There is another important element for Alexandra Palace: Salsbury
was the owner of Buffalo Bill's Wild West Show, which was to perform
in the Palace Theatre a decade later.

By contrast 1881, heralding new hope (springing eternal), had a
busy season of drama. In March — an optimistically early start to the
year — the Theatre hosted a production of WS Gilbert's blank-verse
play Pygmalion And Galatea ("stalls half a crown", "free seats in the
upper gallery").

Gilbert's three-act play was one of several "fairy comedies" in blank
verse that he wrote for John Buckstone and the Haymarket Theatre in
1871. Influenced by the work of James Planche, they were based on
the idea of a character gaining self-knowledge by some supernatural
influence. In this case, it is a sculptor who creates a statue that comes
to life. Pygmalion And Galatea established Gilbert's credentials as a
writer of more than burlesques, and it was his greatest success to that
point — and reputed to have earned him £40, 000 during his lifetime.

It divided critics. According to the Cambridge History Of English
And American Literature: "The satire is shrewd, but not profound ...
but Gilbert's is not the then usual hearty cockney vulgarity." However,

a New York Times review of a production commented: "The play is, from one side, harshly and aggressively disagreeable. Its characters are low, vulgar and selfish."

You pays your money and takes your choice. But it seems ideal for both of Alexandra Palace's demographics.

This production may well have been spun off from Sadler's Wells. One of the actors appears "by permission of Miss Isabel Bateman". The Bateman family, mother and three daughters who were actresses, ran the theatre at that time. The licensee was Mrs Bateman, who had previously run the Lyceum, and she restored the fortunes of Sadlers Wells. But she died in 1881 and the theatre continued to decline, becoming a music hall in the 1890s and a cinema in the early part of the next century, closing in 1915 — some parallels with the Alexandra Palace Theatre.

The Easter Monday production was James Albery's Where's The Cat?, a satire on artistic aestheticism. The lead character is based on Oscar Wilde, and was played by Henry Beerbohm Tree in the original Criterion Theatre production in 1880. This may have been a production by the Charles Wyndham Company, which performed another Albery play at the Alexandra Palace Theatre the following month.

The Tottenham and Edmonton Weekly Herald had some interesting observations on the audience: "It is one of the features of the new management to set a considerable portion of the hall [AP] to the public free of charge, and it was no light matter for those who attempted to enter when the doors were opened.

"In the theatre one gallery was open to all comers, and an hour before the performance of Where's The Cat?, it was crowded, and the audience amused themselves by whistling, shouting, and beating the floor with their feet, keeping time to some popular air."

The founders would hardly have approved — much less the New York Times.

May saw a mix of farce and weightier fare. Tom Taylor's Henry Dunbar or A Daughter's Trials was another adaptation from a novel by Mary Elizabeth Braddon, her most successful work. The theme this time was capital punishment which was widely debated at the time the novel was written in 1864 — public executions had just been abolished.

There was also something to please the founders: two productions of Shakespeare by Charles Kelly's company, Othello at the end of April and The Merchant Of Venice in May. In 1877 Kelly, real name Wardell, married Ellen Terry, after her short marriage to the painter GF Watts and her six-year relationship with the architect Edward Godwin. But

Kelly and Terry had seperated by 1881. In 1878 Terry had joined Henry Irving's company at the Lyceum and after playing Ophelia to Irving's Hamlet, was well on her way to becoming recognised as the leading Shakespearean actress of her day.

At Alexandra Palace, Kelly played Shylock in The Merchant of Venice "with some vigour", with Alma Murray as Portia. Murray also played alongside Irving at the Lyceum. She was associated later with attempts to produce the dramas written by the poets Shelley and Browning, and later performed Galsworthy and Shaw — her correspondence with Shaw was published in the 1920s.

The Daily Programme listed two plays for Wednesday 18 May. The matinee was Pink Dominoes, a "breezy three-act" James Albery farce, performed by the Wyndham Company. Credited as general manager is Frank Beauchamp, and as stage manager Horatio Saker, who also acted one of the main roles. Their respective daughters, Emma Beauchamp and Laura Saker, also acted in the play. All four took similar roles later that month in a production of Betsy, a comedy by Sir Francis (FC) Burnand, showing again how much Victorian theatre was a family affair.

Charles Wyndham was one of the leading actor managers of the late Victorian period. The son of a Liverpool doctor, he trained as a surgeon before turning to the stage. When work for the young actor dried up, he became a brigade surgeon in the Union army in the American civil war, serving at the battles of Fredericksburg, Chancellorsville and Gettysburg. He also once acted with John Wilkes Booth in New York.

Wyndham specialised in melodramas and comedies. In 1876 he took control of the Criterion Theatre and from 1885 on his leading lady was Mary Moore, the wife of James Albery — as widow and widower they married in 1916. Moore also became his partner in ownership of the Criterion and Wyndham's Theatre, opened in 1899. They added the New Theatre in 1903.

Pink Dominoes was followed by an evening performance of James Sheridan Knowles play in five acts, The Hunchback. Actor and writer Knowles was born in Cork and was the cousin of Richard Brinsley Sheridan. He took the lead role in the opening production of The Hunchback at Covent Garden in 1832, but by 1881, he was giving performances of a different kind — to large audiences as a Baptist preacher. Blanche Henri appeared on stage, with her husband Francis Macklin stage managing the production.

Whitsun was in early June, but after a hot start to the month, Whit Monday was cool and wet. Even so, 50,000 people came to the Palace and were guaranteed a spectacular in the theatre. According to Carrington: "The Wood Green Fire Brigade was pressed into service for the performance in the theatre of GR Sims' play The Streets Of London, providing fire engines, horses and complete accessories for the fire scenes."

For once the usually reliable Carrington seems to be wrong in ascribing the play to George Sims. Sims wrote a play called The Lights of London, but this production is almost certainly Boucicault's play, The Streets of London, which does indeed have a finale in which a boarding house is burnt down to destroy evidence of a criminal act — shades of Lady Audley's Secret.

In fact Boucicault's play was first produced in New York in 1857 as The Poor Of New York, but it had several customised productions, including The Poor Of Liverpool and The Streets Of Dublin, as well as the London versions. Exporting and franchising theatre is nothing new.

In early September, the Weekly Herald reported on a performance of Married Life, a play by John Baldwin Buckstone. "The five married couples each jangling in a different and discordant key, always true to life, were well represented in their turn," it judged.

Buckstone, like Wyndham, an actor-manger and comedian, also chalked up 150 plays as a writer. He was born in east London in 1802 and trained as a solicitor, but joined a travelling troupe as an actor in 1821. He first appeared as an actor at the Haymarket in 1833, and Married Life was performed there in 1840.

From 1853, he became the lessee of the theatre and continued to write, albeit at a less hectic pace. He turned the Haymarket into the leading mid-Victorian comedy theatre, with an ensemble including actors such as Andrew Sothern, performing plays by Planche, TW Robertson, Tom Taylor, HJ Byron and WS Gilbert. Illness forced Buckstone to surrender the lease in 1877 and he died in 1879. But reputedly his ghost still makes appearances at the Haymarket — Patrick Stewart reportedly claimed to see his ghost in the wings at a performance of Waiting For Godot.

Caroline Parkes, who appeared in pantomime at the Palace, acted in two farces in a matinee at the beginning of October: An Injured Female — of which no trace can found at the moment; and The Middy Ashore, a one-act farce written by William Bayle Bernard in 1836 — in which our friend Mr TH Friend also took an on-stage role, as a character called Mr Townish.

The evening was rounded off by Tom Taylor's history play, Twixt Axe and Crown or the Lady Elizabeth, set in 1553 in the reign of Queen

Mary. The play was part of a revival in enthusiasm for history plays.

The Macklins returned in mid-October in a matinee performance of WS Gilbert's Sweethearts. And at the end of October Sam Wilkinson, another Alexandra Palace pantomime performer, produced, directed and starred in Thomas J Williams's one-act farce, Turn Him Out.

By the next year, financial problems were again coming back to haunt Alexandra Palace. Perhaps one reflection of this was that almost all the dramatic offerings we have reports of, all between April and July, were farces.

On Easter Monday 1882, a populist bill of fare attracted several full houses. The Weekly Herald reported: "The theatre was but a short time without audiences during the day. In the morning the familiar Boots At The Swan was played, Mr Sam Wilkinson being the 'Boots'. This was followed shortly after by a variety entertainment, in which were Will Griffiths, Lieut Le Ray the ventriloquist, JF Brian, the Great Vance, and others in like character.

"In the afternoon a third audience assembled to see Mr E Terry in A Cure For The Fidgets. And in the evening, GR Sims' Crutch And Toothpick was preceded by another variety entertainment."

Crutch And Toothpick was also directed by Wilkinson.

George R Sims, correctly credited in this case, was of greater interest than suggested by such a farce. Like most farces it lampooned the upper classes, but Sims had a deeper commitment to social criticism — and action. His father was a businessman in the furniture trade, but his mother was president of the Women's Provident League and the daughter of a Chartist. The old Chartist lived with the family when Sims was a child, shaping Sims's early political views. He managed to be a journalist, dramatist, poet and novelist, as well as a bohemian bon vivant, and great sports enthusiast and writer.

Most of his 30 odd plays were adapted from European works and often written with collaborators, including Clement Scott, though most successfully with Henry Pettit. Crutch and Toothpick — the latter referring to a well-fed swell casually picking his teeth — was taken from a French farce by Labiche and was Sims's first big success, in 1879 at the Royalty Theatre. The Melodrama The Lights o' London followed in September 1881 at the Princess's Theatre (too late for it to have been played in June that year at the Alexandra Palace). He made a fortune from his various writings, but mainly gambled it away or gave it to charity.

In 1882, because of his concern for the poor, he was appointed to a study of working-class housing in Southwark, and in 1889 a number of his articles were published in the book How The Poor Live. In 1909 a series of articles he wrote for the Daily Telegraph on child poverty became London At Night. He also wrote for the Daily Mail — Lord Northcliffe was a friend — notably campaigning for the release of a Norwegian, Adolph Beck, who was imprisoned in a case of mistaken identity. The campaign led to the creation of the court of criminal appeal in 1907.

Though remembered still in some radical political circles, as a writer he is mainly known for his much parodied monologue, "It is Christmas Day in the workhouse".

At the end of May, Sam Wilkinson again appears to be at the helm of a double bill of farces, HJ Byron's An Old Story and WE Suter's Give Me My Wife (shades of Ray Clooney), with a similar cast in both, including Henry Monkhouse, Edward Vivian, Gertrude Warden and Sophie Fane.

June 1882 saw several productions, some new to the Palace. In early June there was another production of Coleman's The Jealous Wife, probably in a programme with The Serious Family. Later in the month, the programme switched to Boucicault's London Assurance, and the drama Nine Points Of The Law.

The Serious Family was a comedy with a moral by critic, actor and dramatist Morris Barnett, adapted from the French play Le Mari a la Compagne by Jean-Francois-Alfred Bayard and Jules de Vailly. Its alternative title, La Tartuffe Moderne, indicates its genesis lay even earlier in Moliere. A Spectator review of November 1849, probably of its premiere at the Haymarket, commented:

"The moral purpose of the drama is to show that 'seriousness' at home is likely to produce laxity abroad, and that if a married gentleman hears Exeter Hall mentioned too often by the domestic fireside, he will probably seek amusements of which married ladies ordinarily disapprove."

According to a report in The Dictionary Of Victorian London, Exeter Hall "stands on the north side of the Strand and is dedicated to piety and virtue". So the play is a wonderful piece of double-edged Victorian moralising.

Nine Points Of The Law is another Tom Taylor play, adapted from Clover Cottage, a story by the Irish novelist and journalist, Marmion Savage. The play was first performed at the Olympic Theatre in 1859 and an 1861 production there featured the 12-year-old Ellen Terry.

London Assurance is Boucicault's best known play, a six-act play that was first performed in 1841 at the Theatre Royal Covent Garden and is something of a mid-point — in both senses — between the 18th-century comedies of Sheridan and Goldsmith and those of Oscar Wilde at the end of the 19th century.

It opposes town and country values and the characters include an ageing fop (Sir Harcourt Courtly) engaged to a young heiress (Grace Harkaway), a dissolute son (Charles Courtly), a horse-riding virago (Lady Gay Spanker) and a maid and valet called Pert and Cool. There have been several modern productions, most recently at the National Theatre, with Simon Russell Beale as Sir Harcourt and Fiona Shaw as Lady Gay.

The season ended in early July with a double bill of farces by Harry Paulton's Company: Clodhopper's Fortune — with much the same cast as earlier (Wilkinson, Vivian, Warden, Fane etc); followed by Aunt Charlotte's Maid, with Harry Paulton as Augustus Thomas Fitznoodle, "with songs and imitations". Paulton was a leading comic actor, but also wrote many plays and operas. His most successful work was the comedy Niobe, which is said to have played for over 700 nights in London.

The Alexandra Palace Theatre would then go dark for three years, before the Palace stuttered through more attempts at revival; and then darkness for a decade.

A brief opening for the Palace in 1885 would see another short season in the Theatre. In April, the farces Brother Bill And Me and The Candidate (adapted from the French by JH McCarthy) were performed, and possibly in May, another GR Sims farce, The Member For Slocum. In May there was another outing for Boucicault's Streets of London and in June a performance of WS Gilbert's Pygmalion and Galatea.

But most interesting, Carrington records a production that month of Peril (adopted from Sardou's Nos Intimes), in which two of the greatest actors of the late Victorian period would tread the boards of the Alexandra Palace Theatre: Henry Beerbohm Tree and Lily Langtree. Regrettably, we have so far been unable to find further details

In August 1885 there were productions of The Private Secretary and the popular melodrama East Lynne, both Victorian theatrical classics.

The farce The Private Secretary was adapted by actor-manager Sir Charles Hawtrey not from a French play, but, somewhat exceptionally, from a German book by Gustav von Moser. It premiered in Cambridge in 1883, before transferring to London the next year. It made a fortune for Hawtrey and its main character Reverend Robert Spalding was played by many of the leading actors of the age, including Beerbohm Tree, Frank Thornton and Tyrone Power.

East Lynne was adapted from the 1861 sensation novel by Ellen Wood, and is remembered for its most famous line (which does not appear in the book): "Dead! Dead! And never called me mother!" ("Gone!" in another version). The play was so popular that one critic claimed one version or another was seen by audiences in Britain and North America every week for 40 years.

So far we have only a record of a couple of plays in 1887. East Lynne was performed again — according to Carrington as part of a police fete. The other play performed in early April was a musical comedy called My Sweetheart, a three act musical by William Gill and FG Maeder, which was first produced in America. It was particularly associated with the actress Minnie Palmer who toured extensively with it, including in Australia.

East Lynne was performed again in 1888, a full summer season in the theatre, which included TW Robertson's Caste, and Ben Greet's Players with two Shakespeare productions.

Tom Robertson was another important transitional figure, bringing a new realism and seriousness to mid-Victorian theatre, which is said to have inspired both WS Gilbert and George Bernard Shaw. He came from a theatre family, but was never successful as an actor. He wrote numerous plays, mostly for the Prince of Wales's theatre, dying at only 42 in 1871.

Though most were comedies, more serious offerings such as Caste, and others with suitably pithy titles such as School, MP, and War, brought important changes, both in theme and production. Caste deals with the contemporary preoccupation with class. The son of a French aristocrat marries a dancer and when he is killed in a war, his mother tries to take their child from the poor widow.

In production terms, he was one of the first (along with JR Planche) to take on the role of director ("stage manager") of his own plays — normally that role would have fallen to the actor-manager. He pioneered a naturalistic form dubbed "cup and saucer" theatre because of his efforts to create a normal domestic setting on stage — in Ours, a pudding was made on stage (kitchen sink before its time). He would furnish the stage with the number of chairs a room would normally be expected to have, rather than just enough for the number of actors.

WS Gilbert attended his rehearsals and used what he learnt to direct his own plays and operas, while Shaw called Caste "epoch-making" and referred to Robertson's innovations as a theatrical revolution, though Robertson's plays are rarely performed today.

Also produced at the Theatre in May 1888 was another ground-breaking play: HJ Byron's three-act comedy Our Boys. According to Don Gillan at stagebeauty.net, Our Boys was the first play to run to more than 500 performances — at the Vaudeville from January 1875, setting a new record of 1,362 performances in the Victorian period (and only beaten 15 years later by Charley's Aunt). Improved transport, street lighting and greater prosperity all combined to increase theatre audiences over the century — in the 1820s, passing 100 performances was a landmark.

In June, the Hornsey Journal reports the performance of a play called MD, of which nothing more is known, and a play called Queen Of Fashion, probably by Tom Cannam and JF Preston. The Pickpocket is another play from a German original by Gustav von Moser, this time adapted by George Hawtrey, the brother of Sir Charles Hawtrey.

In July the Theatre would unexpectedly see two Shakespeare productions, As You Like It and A Midsummer Night's Dream. Ben Greet's company had originally planned to perform them outdoors in the Grove area of the park, but it rained. Sir Philip Barling (Ben) Greet was the son of a navy captain, born on HMS Crocodile, who was earmarked by his parents to be a naval officer or a clergyman — but the attractions of the theatre, as so often, were too strong.

In 1886 he started mounting open-air productions through a succession of companies, called, among other things the Woodland Players, or plain Ben Greet Players. As well as returning theatre to the outdoors, he also began a return to Shakespeare's original texts, eschewing the edited and elaborate excesses of mid-Victorian productions. He would return to Alexandra Palace in the new century.

The same month saw another production of the ever-popular Colleen Bawn, and also a play called The Broad Arrow, a sensation piece by Gerald Holcroft, which possibly played to the Alexandra Palace Theatre's strengths in having a railway collision as a key part of the action.

August saw the first production by one of the new generation of playwrights whose work is still performed. Dandy Dick is a farce by Arthur Wing Pinero, author of 59 plays, from serious social dramas such as The Second Mrs Tanqueray, to comedies such as Trelawny Of The Wells. In Dandy Dick an upright clergyman is persuaded to bet on his long-lost sister's race horse, becoming involved in a doping scandal. The play is sometimes performed today and was turned into a Will Hay film in 1935.

East Lynne was again performed, and a melodrama called Current Cash, possibly by a C Clark, which opens in Afghanistan — the second

Anglo-Afghan war ended in 1880 — and involves a soldier's will and a fellow officer's attempts to defraud the widow.

In 1889, as life slowly drained away from the Palace, there was a performance of Boucicault's The Shaughran; a performance of The Balloon by JH Darnley and George Manville Fenn — who wrote 160 novels for boys; and an adaptation for the stage of Aesop's Fables, probably a production by the Comedy Theatre. Then the Theatre would face its darkest hour. The park was to be the only part of Alexandra Palace to see any activity for the next nine years.

When the Palace reopened in 1898, licensing problems for the ageing Theatre meant productions were restricted. There was a revue called Chipps In Japan and, more interestingly, a performance of a spectacular show called The Klondyke Nugget — by Buffalo Bill and his touring company.

This is of double significance. William Cody — Buffalo Bill — was one of the pioneers of flight in this country. He is reported to have flown experimental kites at all his dates, including at Alexandra Palace, all of which was underwritten by The Klondyke Nugget. It was a fitting addition to the tradition of ballooning and parachute jumps held at Alexandra Palace park over the years.

But the final act of the Victorian Theatre was about to unfold off-stage, as private efforts to make Alexandra Palace a success were abandoned and the estate was taken over by a group of local authorities.

Variety and other events
1875-1900

Pantomime, opera and drama in all its forms constitute most of the uses of the Alexandra Palace in the Victorian period, but it was also used for variety performances, dance and some one-off events.

There has been speculation on the unusual shape of the theatre with its long shoe-box shape, including one comparison with the proportions of one of the larger music halls of the period, the Canterbury. But the directors and operators of the Palace throughout the Victorian period were keen to distance themselves from the "low" entertainment of the music hall, with its whiff of scandal, and though variety acts were performed in the theatre, it was usually in the context of a day's entertainment often capped by a more elevated performance such as an opera.

Variety was a more respectable name for the kind of entertainment spawned by the music halls — popular song, comedy, impressionists and all manner of speciality acts from magicians and ventriloquists to juggling and animal acts.

These forms of entertainment have a long lineage going back several centuries to the pleasure gardens on the semi-rural south bank of the Thames, such as at Vauxhall. By the early part of the 19th century, with the rise of an industrial and urban society — and the development of south London — working-class entertainment was increasingly taking place in the saloon bars of public houses, where audiences could eat, drink and smoke while being entertained.

The pre-eminent pub venue was the Grecian Saloon, opened just off the City Road in Islington in 1825 at the Eagle, itself a former tea garden. John Hollingshead, later the proprietor of the Gaiety Theatre, formerly the Strand Music Hall, called it "the wet nurse of the music hall". It is immortalised in the nursery rhyme: "Up and down the City Road / In and out the Eagle / That's the way the money goes / Pop goes the weasel".

By the 1850s, pubs were being pulled down and replaced by purpose-built music halls, the most important being the Canterbury in Lambeth, opened in 1852. By 1865 there were an estimated 32 music halls in London, seating from 500 to 5,000 people. By 1878 this had grown to more than 75, with around 300 smaller venues putting on music hall acts.

Rather than rows of seats, as in a theatre, the music hall had long tables at which members of the audience could eat and drink and smoke, which dictated a much longer auditorium than a traditional theatre that brought the audience much closer to the stage. The Alexandra Palace Theatre is a kind of hybrid, built to music hall proportions, but for a traditionally seated theatre audience — with definitely no eating, drinking or smoking.

How much this was by design is a moot question. Historic theatres expert David Wilmore, a consultant to Alexandra Palace, believes that is was probably not by conscious design. John Johnson, the architect of the second Palace, was not a theatre specialist and probably just adapted to the space available in the north-east corner of the building.

Whatever, it means that the theatre was more suitable for opera, musical theatre and spectacle than for purely spoken drama.

By the late 1870s the number of music halls started to decline because of growing competition and stricter licensing requirements. But the entertainment itself was growing more respectable and being rebranded as variety, with a new generation of more theatre-like venues, epitomised by the London Pavilion rebuilt in 1885. According to Stuart and Park's The Variety Stage, "the gaudy and tawdry music hall of the past gave way to the resplendent 'theatre of varieties' ... with its classic exterior of marble and freestone, its lavishly appointed auditorium and its elegant and luxurious foyers".

Alexandra Palace clearly preferred the "variety" branding, which is how the essentially music hall acts performed in the Palace Theatre were described, when it acknowledged that they actually took place. And mostly they were just part of a programme of events including plays or opera, rather than as stand-alone entertainment.

The first Bank Holiday theatre programme, Whit Monday 1875, includes no variety element (the operetta The Elfin Tree, Brough's farce The Area Belle and the spectacle Minerva).

The first variety act we have a record of was in June 1875 at the Odd Fellows Fete Day, which includes, among a day of events in the Palace and park, a performance by the German conjuror Herr Frikell in the

Theatre. Later in the year, the fete and banquet in commemoration of the Charge of the Light Brigade, on 25 October, included elements of a variety-like programme, with song and poetry recitals between the main performances.

The Whitsun Bank Holiday programme in June 1876 had a decidedly more variety feel about it, with several acts preceding the evening performance of Boucicault's The Colleen Bawn.

The programme was opened by the noted ventriloquist Lieut Walter Cole, with a "comical ventriloquil scene, The Merry Folks". This was followed by two comedy sketches, We All Have Our Little Faults by George Conquest, and a performance by The Great Mackney. This was followed by a "ballet divertissement", the "protean artist" Mr Morris, and a "ballet d'action" by the Payne family — like the Conquests, performers in Alexandra Palace pantomimes.

August Bank Holiday saw a similar programme, with Conquest in Chopsticks And Spikins, followed by The Great Mackney and Mr Morris "and his mystic changes", all sandwiched between two dance performances: Lizzie Simms in a Ballet Of All Nations to start; and a comic ballet, The Young Miller or The Scamp Of The Village, mounted by Monsieur and Madame Espinosa (also involved in the AP pantomimes).

The Great Mackney (though not so great as to leave more than a trace) performed at August Bank Holiday 1877, between the "musical absurdity" Crazed and the "laughable protean sketch" Day After The Fair, with the evening rounded off again with The Colleen Bawn. Mackney was a singer who played the fiddle, and also appeared "blacked up" as a minstrel.

A variety programme — in fact the first use of the word in the Palace literature — was advertised for a weekday afternoon later that month. The A Division of Police Glee Class was billed to open with two "glees" — song and poetry recitals — Desolate is the Dwelling of Morna and Comrades in Arms, with Mr FJ Hunt conducting; followed by Macfarren's song, The Beating of My Own Heart, sung by Miss Emily Mott, a recitation of The Charge of the Light Brigade, and Mott singing Wrighton's Sing Me An English Song.

The "glees" were followed by Offenbach's operetta A Mere Blind, and Suter's one-act farce Waiter At The Eagle, in which George Conquest was billed to play Jenkins, the waiter.

Also advertised that day, for 6pm, were the Metropolitan Police Minstrels, performing songs including Cling to Those That Cling to You, sung by Sgt JB Smart; The Darling of Our Home (Sgt HR Wilson); the comic song The Buckles on Her Shoe (Sgt WT Wren); and I Long for My Home in Kentuck (Sgt C Marriner). The whole was rounded off by the company singing the Anvil Chorus from Il Trovatore.

The finale after a short interval was billed to include Alice Where Art Thou (Sgt JG Littlechild); an American jig performed by Constable J Haines; and the company performing a "laughable farce", Barnum's Speculation. The conductor was billed as Mr D Smith, inspector.

Song plays a central role in music hall and variety entertainment. Originally, the songs derived from folk song and popular drama, but increasingly took on more contemporary and humorous subject matter. Influences came from far and wide, as instanced by the programme above. In the 1840s, in the US, Stephen Foster adapted the Black American spiritual into a new form, the minstrel song, and the influence soon spread around the world. Continental European music also fed into the genre, particularly the jig, polka and waltz. What we now think of as music hall songs would not develop until the late 1860s and 1870s.

A variety entertainment was reported by the Weekly Herald in February 1878, as a benefit for the Turkish victims of the Russo-Turkish war. The paper refers to "the long list of items in the programme being contributed gratuitously by the artistes concerned" adding, "in the afternoon, the entertainments passed off quietly, although successfully, the variety attractions in the theatre having the preference". Live Aid, 19th-century style.

Among the acts were "Mr Harry Jackson's imitations of Messers Sothern, Irving, Toole and Clarke; Mr Lionel Brough's 'Muddle-Puddle Porter'; Mr George Conquest's parrot, from the Grecian pantomime; and a scene from the Pink Flamingoes, by the Criterion company,." Herbert Campbell also sang.

The AP programme of events advertises a "variety" performance in the Theatre for Easter Monday 1878, with, once again Walter Cole's Merry Folks (a "grand ventriloqual, mimical and biloquial entertainment"), with characters including Tommy Treadlehoyle "a jolly old Lancashre Lad", Maggie Macdougall, "a braw Scotch lassie", and Mr James Anderson, "the insolvent lodger — 'Oh! my poor legs'". Also on the bill was the Rowella family (also AP pantomime artists), and the Gaiety theatre burlesque, Little Doctor Faust.

At the end of May a similar bill included Merry Folks, Mackney's Originalities — "vocal, instrumental and saltatorial capabilities, topical illusions, paraphrases, imitations with peculiar effects etc". The evening performance was the comedy Paul Pry.

In 1879 the Majiltons, Charles, Frank and Marie appeared in their "screaming dramatic performance" Round the Clock, with the "infant Salvini (aged five and a half years)" reciting "The Charge Of The Light Brigade or Good News From Ghent" in between the acts.

In 1880 and 1881, dance and ballet seems to find favour in the Theatre. On two Saturdays in June there were dance programmes, courtesy of Augustus Harris at the Drury Lane Theatre. On 12 June, there were two performances of a programme called National Dances, which included the Styrian dance, Hungarian dance, Bolero and Tarantella. This was repeated the next Saturday, but was followed by a "grand ballet d'action", Les Sirenes.

Prominent as a performer was "Mdlle Palladino". Emma Palladino, who achieved some prominence in the 1880s, was the daughter of a dancer at La Scala and trained there. She toured America before making her London debut at Her Majesty's in 1879, beginning a career that lasted until the end of the century. One contemporary review describes her as "a vigorous and skilful demonstrator of her art", adding: "This lady, too, appears to be thoroughly genial, and the genuine smile which pervades her features as she executes her difficult gyrations adds a pleasure to the performance."

Despite her elevated status, she also appeared as principal dancer in Drury Lane's 1882 pantomime of Cinderella, with other AP artists Herbert Campbell and Kate Vaughan.

In June 1881, the Lauris, John, George and Miss Fanny, much involved in AP pantomimes, mounted a grand ballet, The Fire Fiend, attributed to "the Lauris and the Famous Fred Girard". (Mayerbeer's opera Dinorah was the evening performance.)

In August it was the turn of another pantomime choreographer, Katti Lanner, who presented Une Fete Cosmopolite, a "grand ballet divertissement in two tableaux" by pupils of the National School for Dancing, before an evening performance of Gilbert and Sullivan's Trial By Jury.

Easter Monday 1882 and the Tuesday after saw another mixed programme of comedy drama (Boots At The Swan and Crutch And Toothpick) and variety. The AP programme of events details 11 "variety entertainment" acts on the Tuesday, including comic vocalist Will Griffiths, another ventriloquist, Lieut le Ray (why are ventriloquists lieuts?), Nelly Wilson, vocalist and dancer, Olive Rose, fire rope dancer, The Angel Trio of Gymnasts and The Great Vance.

Alfred Vance was one of the first stars of the music hall, though always linked to his better-known rival, George Leybourne — Champagne Charlie. (A 1944 film of the same name featured Tommy Trinder as Leybourne and Stanley Holloway as Vance.)

The typical music hall song that we still recognise today (Any Old Iron, Boiled Beef And Carrots etc) consists of verses sung by the performer and a chorus with an easily remembered melody, which the audience joins in. The first such songs seem to have been written to promote the alcoholic wares of the music hall owners. Champagne Charlie, sponsored by fizz maker Moet and Chandon in 1867, would become the first big music hall success. Vance followed with Clicquot, Clicquot, a paean to a rival brand.

Both were what became known as lion comiques, artists who dressed up as toffs, singing about swilling champagne, going to races and living the life of a swell. In fact, Leybourne was a labourer from Newcastle and Vance originally a solicitor's clerk. And aping the lifestyle didn't turn out too well for them. Leybourne died in poverty in 1884 of exhaustion and probably alcohol, while Vance died on stage (literally) in 1888 at the age of 49.

Champagne Charlie's easily remembered tune became a Salvation Army hymn, Bless His Name, He Sets Me Free, and prompted the famous remark by the Army's founder, William Booth, "why should the devil have all the best tunes".

The Tottenham and Edmonton Weekly Herald reports in August 1882 "variety entertainments" by "the leading individuals who appear at the London music halls". No details are given, but the Palace would not have been best pleased with the latter description.

An undated AP programme of events, most likely from 1885, lists a whole day's programme, which includes the farce Brother Bill And Me, the comedy The Candidate, and a burlesque, Little Lohengrin, interspersed with "variety entertainment", including the comic Harry Wyndham, soprano Nellie Challice and "The Original Liskard (the great musical momus)".

Also on the bill was "An Aesthetic Quadrille by Mr C Hilt, Mesdames Beresford, Nieumann and Grey", W Bint (comic), Florrie Florence (serio-comic), Atroy (equilibrist) and — to show the ecumenical nature of "variety" — an address by the Tichborne Claimant, the cause celebre in a famous Victorian court case.

The brief, final swansong of the Palace under private ownership, at the end of the 1890s, is not so much variety as a ragbag. April 1898 offered a two-day programme of "grand vaudeville and variety entertainments", interspersed with "Dioramic views. Musically illustrated."

In September a full day's programme presented an afternoon performance of Chipps In Japan, a "musical comical Japanese sketch",

Sheet music cover — © The British Library Board. All rights reserved. Shelf mark: H.1561.(8.)

featuring "native musicians, oriental dancers, fire eater, tim-tam players, Soudanese performers, the celebrated Levy family from Algiers"; while in the evening was the last great hippodrama: The Klondyke Nuggett, written and arranged by SF Cody (Buffalo Bill).

The cast (including Miss Lela Cody) was "supported by trained horses, who will perform in their respective scenes ... Also five highly bred horses and five mules".

Despite the odds, the Palace had always stubbornly hung on, but there was only to be one final performance of greatest hits. In July 1900 there was a mixed programme of excerpts from Maritana; a "magnificent series of animated war pictures" (early film, perhaps?); and a ballad concert with Iver McKay singing Sullivan's Mary Morison and Wallace's Let Me Like A Soldier Fall; and Marie Elba singing Lovers' Quarrel and Foolish Men.

The series of ultimately foolish men who tried with hope against experience to make the Palace a success had finally fallen on their collective sword and by September a board of trustees was supervising the transfer of the Palace into public hands, under a consortium of local authorities.

Afterword

The transfer of the Alexandra Palace and Park to the public sector, enshrined in the 1900 act of parliament and later consolidated under the 1985 act, guaranteed a future for the great Victorian pleasure palace so that it remained open to the public, in some fashion, throughout its subsequent history, apart from the two world wars. Which is not to say that it was a success. The daunting economics of a seven and half acre palatial building on a suburban hilltop provided continuing problems and often need for public subsidy.

The Alexandra Palace Theatre underwent a revival after 1900 and opera and theatre returned to the stage. But already mass entertainment was changing from live performance to the new medium of cinema and the Theatre was not immune. In many ways the period from 1900 up until the first world war was the most successful in the Theatre's history. It installed a projection room at the back of the lower balcony (still there today), and turned increasingly to film exhibition as the popular audience grew — though live performances of theatre and opera also continued.

The Palace was closed at the start of the first world war and soon after was used as a reception centre for Belgian refugees fleeing the fighting and occupation. It then became an internment camp for "enemy aliens", those of German and Turkish descent considered as potential enemies in the heightened tensions of the war. Those interned included artists and musicians and the internees put on performances in the Theatre.

The building was left in a poor state after the war and the trustees who now ran the Palace had to haggle with the government over reparations. Some money was eventually provided, most of it spent on refurbishing the Theatre by the new general manager, W McQueen Pope. However, the rather staid, rigid proscenium arch Theatre which reopened in 1922 failed to find an audience and was soon under financial pressure. In 1923, the Theatre was leased to Archie Pitt, the husband of Gracie Fields to rehearse shows and reviews destined for the West

End, though some theatrical and operatic performances did continue, mainly by semi-professional groups.

In the financially constrained years of the 1930s, the Palace was badly affected and was saved by another new nascent medium of popular entertainment: television. In 1935, the BBC took a lease on the east end of the building to set up trials of its new television service, which started broadcasting to a small audience in November 1936. It seems the BBC did draw up plans for using the Theatre for programme production, but these were never implemented — probably because the technical limitations of the equipment demanded smaller spaces. So it became a storage space for scenery until the BBC left.

The television service was closed in 1939 along with the Palace for the duration of the second world war. The television transmission tower was used to confuse the radar of German bombers attacking the capital (possibly the reason the investment in television — a similar technology to radar — was made in the first place).

The television service reopened in 1946, but already the BBC was laying plans to move general programme production of the expanding medium to a new centre at Lime Grove. That transferred in 1954, leaving the news operation, until that too moved in 1969. The new Open University broadcasting unit remained until that too moved in 1981.

After the BBC packed up and left, the Theatre fell into increasing dereliction. It survived the fire of 1980 which devastated the central and western parts of the building (though the green rooms and backstage facilities were destroyed). But plans to turn it into a recording studio under the 1985 redevelopment plan were never implemented because the insurance money ran out (echoes of 1873).

In 1996 the building was listed grade II by English Heritage, largely because of the survival of the Victorian wooden stage. In the following years, the trustees, with the help of some grants from English Heritage re-roofed the Theatre to make it wind and water tight, and began a series of repairs, culminating in reflooring the foyer to replace the wooden floor ripped out because of dry rot in the 1980s. With safe access restored, a Friends group was set up to help promote plans to refurbish and re-use the Theatre, with a number of small events being put on each year in both the auditorium and foyer.

Safety concerns over the ceiling meant the auditorium was closed again in 2009, only reopening after repair work to structural beams in December 2013. That month, a short adaptation of Dickens' Christmas Carol became the first production to be performed from the stage of the Theatre to an audience in the auditorium for almost 80 years — to great enthusiasm of the small crowd who braved the icy conditions.

The Theatre is now the largest element in a £25m regeneration project for the whole east end of the building, including the former BBC studios and East Court, which is currently (October 2014) in the second stage of development. If Heritage Lottery funding for the main project is granted in 2015, the Theatre could be reborn as a mulit-use performance space by the end of 2017.

Sources and acknowledgements

There are two main sources for the information on performances and developments in the Theatre: the Tottenham and Edmonton Weekly Herald (1873-1900) and the Alexandra Palace Daily Programmes (1877-1898), both series of which are in the Haringey Archives at Bruce Castle Museum. Further information has come from contemporary issues of the Hornsey Journal (1879-1898) and some other local newspapers; The Alexandra Palace Programme of Arrangements 1875-76; and the book, Fete and Banquet in Commemoration of the Charge of the Light Brigade, 1875; also at Bruce Castle.

RC Carrington's Alexandra Park and Palace — A History has been the main source for the general history of the Palace and also for some theatre performances for which we have not yet found detailed information in programmes or newspaper reviews.

Wherever possible we have indicated these sources in the text. In general, if not indicated, the source of the information on particular performances is the Tottenham and Edmonton Weekly Herald.

In addition, information was sourced from The Alexandra Palace Programmes of Arrangements 1873-74 and 1876-77; Programme and Book of Words of the Great National Holiday Festival, Whit Monday, May 17th 1875; Programme and Book of Words of the Balfe Memorial Festival, Saturday July 29th 1876; at The British Library, London.

Librettos of Harlequin The Yellow Dwarf or The King of the Goldmines, by the Brothers Grinn, London: RK Burt and Co (1875); and Turko the Terrible or The Great Princess Show, by William Brough, London: RK Burt (1876); provided information about scenes, characters, actors, creative and technical personnel of these pantomimes; and are from the Pettingell Collection, Special Collections & Archives, Templeman Library, University of Kent, Canterbury, UK.

The Puss in Boots or the Butterflies' Ball and Grssshoppers' Feast libretto, by Frank Stainforth, London (probably 1880) in Senate House Library, University of London, augmented understanding of that pantomime. The informative article on the first performances in the second Theatre from The Era, 9 May 1875, is from the British Newspaper Archive.

Most of the information on performers, writers, producers, directors and so on has been from a variety of sources such as the Dictionary of National Biography, the East End Theatre Archive and Wikipedia. Sometimes information on less well-known artists or works has had to be pieced together from brief references in newspaper articles from as far afield as Australia and New Zealand. We hope to provide fuller referencing of sources in a later edition.

We would like in particular to acknowledge the help of and thank all the staff at Bruce Castle Museum; staff at the Special Collections & Archives, Templeman Library, University of Kent; and at The British Library.

Thanks also to Tim Willmott for his patient work on the production of this book and Wendy Willmott for proof-reading. Any remaining errors are the authors' alone.

List of illustrations

Front cover The Theatre auditorium today
P16 First Alexandra Palace — ground and gallery floor plans
P25 Second Alexandra Palace — plan
P30 Plan of Alexandra Palace and Park in the AP Daily Programme, 23 December 1879
P38 Harlequin The Yellow Dwarf libretto title page
P51 Cobweb Caves and Spider's Glen from the Harlequin The Yellow Dwarf libretto
P54 Princess Allfair and the Yellow Dwarf from the Harlequin The Yellow Dwarf libretto
P58 Turko the Terrible — cast list
P87 Maritana libretto (1888)
P97 AP Daily Programme, 8 June 1878 — Led Astray
P104 AP Daily Programme, 25 June 1878 — Hamlet
P125 Sheet music cover (1871) of song sung by The Great Vance
Back cover Detail of the Theatre ceiling today